Trouble in the Hills

Trouble in the Hills

 *Helaine Becker*

Fitzhenry & Whiteside

Published in Canada by Fitzhenry & Whiteside, 195 Allstate Parkway,
Markham, Ontario L3R 4T8
Published in the United States by Fitzhenry & Whiteside, 311 Washington
Street, Brighton, Massachusetts 02135
www.fitzhenry.ca   godwit@fitzhenry.ca
10 9 8 7 6 5 4 3 2 1
Library and Archives Canada Cataloguing in Publication
Becker, Helaine, 1961-
Trouble in the hills / Helaine Becker.
ISBN 978-1-55455-174-3
I. Title.
PS8553.E295532T76 2011   jC813'.6   C2011-905805-7
Publisher Cataloging-in-Publication Data (U.S)
Becker, Helaine.
Trouble in the hills / Helaine Becker.
[208] p. : cm.
Summary: Following a fight with his father, Cam takes to the hills surrounding
his small mountain community, and after an error in judgement leads to a
serious mountain biking accident, Cam must make his way back home over
the cold inhospitable terrain while eluding kidnappers and drug runners.
ISBN: 978-1-55455-174-3 (pbk.)
1. Adventure – Juvenile fiction. I. Title.
[Fic] dc22   PZ7.B325Tr 2011
Fitzhenry & Whiteside acknowledges with thanks the Canada Council for
the Arts, and the Ontario Arts Council for their support of our publishing
program. We acknowledge the financial support of the Government of
Canada through the Canada Book Fund (CBF) for our publishing activities.

Canada Council   Conseil des Arts
for the Arts   du Canada

ONTARIO ARTS COUNCIL
CONSEIL DES ARTS DE L'ONTARIO

ANCIENT FOREST™ FRIENDLY

Preserving our environment
Fitzhenry & Whiteside Limited chose to print the pages of this
book on recycled paper and saved these resources[1]:

energy	water	greenhouse gases	solid waste
1 million BTUs	55,045 L	1,463 kg	418 kg

32
trees were saved
for our forests

Printed by Webcom Inc. on
Legacy Hi-Bulk Natural 100% post-consumer waste.

[1]Estimates were made using the Environmental Defense Paper Calculator.

FSC
www.fsc.org
MIX
Paper from
responsible sources
FSC® C004071

Cover design by Daniel Choi
Cover image courtesy of Jim Semlor/Wikimedia Commons
Interior design by Comm Tech Unlimited
Printed in Canada

Dedication

This book is dedicated to the BC Librarians Association, which invited me to do a reading tour in the Kootenays in 2008. It was on that trip that the idea for this book was born.

I'd also like to thank Leanne Strang, Grand Forks librarian extraordinaire, for her hel with plotting; the Grand Forks Cycling Club for providing details that helped make scenes of mountain biking in the recion as accurate as Possible, and Dr. Shari L. Forbes, the Director of Forensic Science and Associate Professor of Forensic Science and Chemistry at the University of Ontario Institute of Technology for help in understanding how cave environments affet decomposition of various materials.

And a huge thanks to Mahtab Narsimhan, not only for being a kind and astute first reader, but for helping me to make sure Samira's voice and mannerisms rang true.

1

The *whomp! whomp! whomp!* of the choppers was deafening. They loomed overhead like giant man-eating insects, ready to pounce.

"*You are surrounded. Surrender peacefully and you will not be harmed,*" an amplified voice commanded. It seemed like it was coming from everywhere at once.

Cam instinctively held his breath so as not to betray his presence. Not that anyone could hear him amid the chaotic roar of the machines.

He crouched low, trying to flatten himself into the meadow. There was almost nowhere left to go; their only chance was the creek. Once there, they could make their way along its sheltered banks, hidden by the willows that lined its edge. Then, maybe, they could get to safety.

But where was Dakota? He should have been right behind them. *Why couldn't that guy* ever *stick with the program, not even this once?*

Samira leaned against him, trying to catch her breath. Her chin was digging into the hollow above his collarbone, but Cam didn't even let himself so much as twitch. He knew she needed rest. She'd been through ten times more than he had.

"We have to go now," Cam whispered.

Her reply was just a ragged sigh.

Cam reached for her hand. She laced her fingers through his and squeezed them tight.

"The searchlights," he pressed. "We're not going to be able to avoid them much longer."

"You don't need to do this for me, you know. You don't owe me anything," she said.

"Maybe not," he replied. "But I'm not leaving you. Or Dakota." With the back of his hand, he brushed a wisp of damp hair off her forehead. "Come on. We have to get down to the creek. Now."

He didn't wait for the next sweep of the lights. Keeping his body low to the ground, he started to run, pulling Samira along with him. He kept his mind firmly on his goal—reaching the creek. He could hardly make it out; it was just a dark line against the even darker lines of hills and sky. Samira would never get there on her own.

The search lights cut another broad swath through the field. Cam deked to avoid them, but even so, this time they came scarily close.

The noise, the wind, and the blinding lights all made Cam dizzy and disoriented. He couldn't tell if the throb in his chest was the reverb from the relentless beat of the chopper blades, or from the hammering of his own heart. He glanced up to check his bearings and wound up looking right into a high-intensity beam. Bright pink spots flared in his vision. Everything else went black.

"Cam? Those lights! I can't see a thing!" Samira wailed.

"Me neither. Hang in there. We're close. Just follow me and stay low!"

Swearing softly to himself, Cam dropped to his knees. Now they would have to *feel* their way to the creek.

Tough grass slapped him in the face and filled his mouth with grime as he crawled commando style. He wouldn't have thought the world could hold even more terror when an ATV appeared out of nowhere. It swooped across the field at top speed.

Cam shrank into himself, willing himself to be invisible. The ATV seemed about to pass them by when it made a sharp turn. Suddenly, its intense headlights shone right on Cam and Samira. They'd been caught!

"Run!" shouted Cam, knowing even as the words escaped his lips that it was too late. The ATV was bearing down on them. It was going to run them over!

There was nothing more to do. It was all over. Cam pulled Samira to him and covered her body with his own. He closed his eyes and waited for the huge wheels of the ATV to crush them like roadkill.

The ATV roared past.

"What the—!" Cam gasped. *He had to have seen us!* he thought. The wheels had missed them only by inches!

Squinting, Cam watched the ATV career recklessly across the field, gears screaming as the engine was pushed to the max. The choppers swooped and dove overhead, their lights swinging crazily this way and that. Their furious blades battered Cam with blasts of hot wind. The gusts flattened the grass and flung stinging sand into Cam's face.

Then, the search beams began to converge on the ATV.

As each searchlight latched onto it, the ATV's yellow paint seemed to glow brighter and brighter. To Cam, it looked like a chariot of fire against the night sky.

Standing tall on the machine, the driver was just an anonymous black shape silhouetted by the searchlights. He held his arms out to the sides like a crazy man.

One search beam caught the driver full on. His face was suddenly illuminated. Cam heard Samira gasp beside him. It was Dakota!

Dakota's eyes locked onto Cam's. One nanosecond of perfect understanding passed between them. Dakota smiled that wacked-out smile of his. Then he flipped Cam the bird.

Cam heard Dakota gun the engine. The ATV roared off, away from the creek. The searchlights stayed with it, tracking Dakota's path across the pasture.

"Run! Now!" Cameron shouted. Samira and Cam both leapt to their feet. Shielded by the darkness, they sprinted toward the creek.

Cam had never run so hard in all his life. At last, the deep shadows ahead of them gained definition. They separated into individual shapes—the trees and bushes at the creek's edge. With lungs burning and every muscle on fire, Cam crashed through the tangled shrubs. Samira was right behind him. The moist fragrance of the creek bed rose up to welcome them. *They'd made it!*

Although the draping tree branches seemed to offer them shelter, the bank itself was treacherous. It was steep, pocked with exposed roots and wobbly stones, and slippery with ooze and mud. But there was no time to plan a careful descent. They were still far from safe.

Cam hurtled down the slope, sometimes running, sometimes sliding, sometimes flailing wildly. When he finally skittered to a stop at the bottom, winded and shaky with the effort, he was relieved to see Samira there, too. She'd slid on her bum down the slope.

He was just about to help Samira to her feet when a staccato burst of gunfire ripped through the night. There was a flash of white. A terrifying *whoosh* tore through the air, and a concussive wall of wind slammed into Cam, sending him staggering backwards.

Sudden comprehension coursed through him.

He cradled his head in his hands. "No," he yelled. "No! No!"

Samira was instantly on her feet at his side. She gripped his arm.

"No! Don't look!" she begged.

Cam shrugged her hand away. Filled with dread, he scrambled back up the bank. He peered over the lip of the ravine. What he saw made him want to puke.

Cam fought down the screams that rose in his throat. Every instinct in his body urged him to run to Dakota, to save him.

"No," shouted Samira, her voice now wrapped in steel. "There's nothing we can do to help him anymore. We must get away. Now." She clambered up beside him and put a restraining hand on his arm.

Cam took a deep, shuddering breath. *Jesus, Dakota,* he thought. *Why'd you* always *have to be such an a-hole?*

Resigned, Cam let himself slide back down the bank. He wiped his muddy palms on his backside and took Samira's hand in his. Together, they waded into the river. As the water foamed and splashed around his knees, the tears began to course down his cheeks.

2

Three days earlier

His father's eyes shot dark bolts of fury.

Great, Cam thought. *He's home five frigging minutes and I'm already in the doghouse.*

Cam kept fiddling with his iPod, pretending not to notice the man-mountain glowering at him from his bedroom doorway. But a sudden rime of sweat prickled his scalp, and his right eyelid twitched.

For the hundredth time since Easter, Cam wished his dad had never come home, that he would just stay away. Whenever he showed up, Cam's whole life went Code Orange.

His father cleared his throat. "Is what your mother tells me true?"

Cam shrugged one shoulder, kept his eyes on his iPod. "Sure, whatever," he mumbled.

"Don't you sass me, Cameron!" his father said, his voice like barbed wire.

A hot flame shot up the back of Cam's neck. "How should I know what she told you? It's not like I was sitting between you two lovebirds as you compared notes on your 'problem child.'" *Again.* The words left a sour taste in Cam's mouth.

13

His dad didn't reply. He just waited, letting his patented 'make-'em-squirm' silence stretch for eons.

And it worked—boy, did it work. Cam wanted to blurt something—*anything*—out, just to break that dead air. It was as if the silence itself was urging him to go for it: *Come on, buddy, step out on the tarmac. Today's your lucky day. This time, you'll say the magic words and catch a ride outta here.*

Yeah, right. As if anything he came up with would get him a pass. With his dad, there was no way you could ever be right. If Cam spoke up, he'd just be dead meat that much faster.

So Cam willed himself to be still, to hold his tongue and wait his dad out. Anxiety, that old, cold snake, twisted round and round in his gut.

"So you want to play that game, Mr. Smart Alec?" his father said. One of his massive knuckles drummed the door frame. "Fine. Just so there's no mistake, here's the 411: Your mother said that you've been neglecting your chores. And that yesterday Stargate got out of the barn and halfway down to Carson Road because you'd left the gate open."

He stopped and waited—again. "So? Got anything to say? What's your excuse this time, Cameron?"

Cam didn't answer. What was the point? Instead, Cam just sat there, staring blindly at the touchscreen, silently praying to himself: *just go away, just go away, just go away…*

His dad stormed through the doorway and into the room. *Incoming! Incoming! Duck for cover…!*

He yanked the iPod from Cam's ears.

"What were you thinking?" his father laced into him. "Or

14

do you not bother to think at all? Is it just empty air whizzing around in there between those…ear-things?"

Cam's ear hurt like a bugger, but he didn't let himself show it. He wouldn't give his dad the satisfaction.

His father shook his head and, with a snarl of disgust, turned away.

"No—don't answer that. I already know the answer."

Cam felt his cheeks go hot. He wanted to hit something, anything. He wanted to leap to his feet, overturn his bed, and roar like a cartoon villain. He wanted to crack his crappy D-I-Y desk over his dad's head 'til that self-satisfied, know-it-all smirk on his dad's face got wiped away once and for all.

But Cam just raised his eyes to his dad's. From between clenched teeth, Cam said, "Welcome home, Dad. So nice to have you back."

The next instant, his father was in his face. "Don't you go and lay your bad attitude on me, kiddo. You're expected to do your part while—"

"You mean do *your* part, Dad," Cameron shot back. "Stargate's not my horse, she's yours. Don't make it my fault just 'cause you're never around to look after her."

Us.

"So that's what this is about then?" his dad replied. "You know I'm busting my ass out there, Cam. Do you think I like being gone half of every mon—?"

He stopped himself midstream. He pivoted on his heel and was halfway out the door before he turned back to Cam. With his dark eyes glittering from beneath thundercloud brows, he said,

"I don't have to justify myself to you. I got my job to do. You don't like it? Tough. It's not about to change any time soon. And whether you like it or not, you got a job, too—and you know what it is."

Cam snorted. "Yeah, yeah, yeah." He chanted in a falsetto, "'Holding down the fort.'" Under his breath, he added, "Much thanks I get for it."

His father slammed the flat of his hand down on Cam's desk. The pencils jumped in their holder.

"Right—I forgot—you're the one who's so hard done by. Having your meals cooked for you, your clothes washed for you, nothing for you to do but bugger off with that no-account pal of yours. So you have to lend a helping hand to your mom now and then. Is that really too much to bear? Go ahead and moan about your piss-poor life, then. I don't care. Just remember that people were counting on you, you piece of—and that you let them down. Again."

His father's eyes bored into him. "Consider yourself grounded, son. Plan on nothing but chores and homework until you learn the meaning of responsibility. And if you can quit your boo-hoo-hooing for two seconds, maybe you'll find out what it means to step up and be a man. It would damn well be about time."

The rebuke hit Cam like a right jab to the gut. He felt himself get smaller and smaller, shrinking into himself until there was nothing of him left but a tiny knot of pain.

Hang on. Hold it together, cowboy, he thought.

"Have you anything to say for yourself?" Cam's father said. When Cam didn't respond, his father added coldly, "Didn't think so."

Cam heard the thud of his father's retreating footsteps as if from the bottom of a well.

With his father gone, Cam let himself sink back into his bed pillows, drained. He finally allowed himself to rub his sore ear. He tossed the iPod onto his nightstand, and something white went bouncing off under the bed. One of the earbuds.

Cam ignored it. What did it matter? He curled into a ball, his face to the wall.

It was a piece of crap anyway, just like everything else in his life.

Just like him.

3

Cam's Vans made a soft *whoof* as he landed in the dirt beneath his bedroom window. He took a few tentative steps and listened again. Still no sign of his father.

As he came around the corner of the house, he could see the rugged sweep of the mountains that lay to the south and west of the farm. In the northwest, on Mount Observation, he could just make out the dark zigzag of the trail he and Dakota had nicknamed 'Geronimo' way back when.

If only he were out there right now, he could forget all this B.S. When you're hurtling down a mountain at forty-five clicks, with nothing between you and brain death but a Crappy Tire helmet, there's no time to worry about pain-in-the-butt parents. There's no time to think at all. You just react, with nerves and muscles firing together in a perfect symphony of adrenalin and speed.

His bike's scratched, muddy frame was leaning casually against the carport's wall. Cam put his hand on the seat, patting the saddle as if the bike were his trusty steed. He couldn't help but remember all of the good times he'd had on that bike. Last summer had been a serious blast, him and Dakota bombing around in the hills. Even that time they crashed and burned, racing each other down Mount Thimble, had been totally great.

"Definitely worth the road rash!" Dakota had crowed, the blood from his split lip outlining his teeth in red.

Cam had walked with a limp for almost a week after that awesome run, but yeah, it had been worth it. If only Dakota hadn't gone AWOL when they started at Grand Forks High. "I got bigger fish to fry now, bro," he had said to Cam. Dakota had pointed his finger like a gun and winked before swaggering off with some kids Cam didn't know.

The heck with him, Cam said to himself. *You don't need Dakota or anyone else to get out in the hills, find a wailin' single track, and let 'er rip.*

Cam shook his head. He didn't get it, though. What did Dakota see in those guys? So they were "cool." Big deal. They didn't ever *do* anything. They just stood around under the big shade tree in front of the school, reeking of weed and thinking nobody noticed.

Mountain-biking: now that was Cam's idea of a good time. Pounding his way up a trail, no matter how hard it was, seemed way easier than trying to find his way through the twists and turns of everyday life. On his bike, it was as if he were in tune with the spirit of the mountain.

He checked the position of the sun and nodded sharply to himself. A good two to three more hours still before it set for real. He could get all the way up to the top of the trail and be back before supper. No one would even know he had gone.

4

He stepped onto his left pedal and pushed off. His heart lightened at the sound of gravel *shhhhushing* under his wheels.

There wasn't a car or truck in sight on Carson Road, so he carved wide, swinging turns that looped from one side of the asphalt to the other. It made him feel like he was flying, the tethers that held him to Earth loosed and flapping like wings.

Still less than halfway across town, he could smell the Kettle River. It was high at this time of year, and the scent of the mountains and moss were carried straight into town on its rushing current. The promise of summer—better times—tickled his nose.

His favourite part of every ride was that moment when town and all the people and things in it—the cars, the noise, everything—dropped away. The trees would close in and it would feel like he had disappeared into another world. His heartbeat, even the rhythm of his own breath, would feel *right*. In and out, over and over again, the cycle of time and life repeating endlessly in a perfect loop. And there, he'd be part of it—hey, he'd be at the *centre* of it—each perfectly timed downstroke of the pedal, each powerful surge of blood through his veins, echoing the pulse of the mountain.

His teeth clacked against each other and his spine rattled as he slalomed across the footbridge's rickety slats. Beneath him, the water rushed and swirled, high and cold.

On the other side, a dirt trail wound through stands of straggly willows and cottonwoods. Their branches were bare, and their grey, gnarled fingers rubbed against each other with a drybones sound. But Cam could see the swelling of buds all along their lengths, barely restraining their mad burst into leaf and flower. *Any day now*, they promised. *Our turn is coming.*

The trail itself was wide, flat, and smooth, covered with a papery mulch of dead leaves. It sent up a soft fragrance that reminded him of hay.

Cam pedaled hard as the trail began to climb. A warm ache pulsed through his legs with each pedal stroke. It felt good: that hot, physical pain that blanked out everything else. He barely noticed when the soft mulch under his wheels was replaced by layers of crunching needles. He'd become nothing but legs and guts and breath.

The trail was steep and twisting, punctuated with rocks and criss-crossed with deadfall. He'd have to look sharp if he didn't want to find himself sliding down the trail bass-ackwards, wearing his handlebars like frigging antlers.

His thoughts narrowed to a simple litany of commands. *Jump, turn, slide…pedal hard! Hop and corner, hop and corner again, dig, dig, dig!* He barely registered the cold steel against his fingertips, or how his chest, held low and open, burned with the effort of the climb. His legs were self-propelled pistons. His glutes were a fiery furnace, stoked to the max.

It took every ounce of his effort to keep his gears from slipping and his wheels from catching in the groove of the track, but Cam kept at it. Then, at last, he reached the crest of the trail. A few more wobbly pedal strokes and *YES!* He was there! His quads were killing, sweat was streaming into his eyes, and he was blowing like a humpback, but he'd made it—top o' the rock. For Cam, this was heaven, or as close to heaven as a misfit like him would ever get, anyway.

Cam hopped off his bike, stretched and took a few slack-limbed steps toward where the flat table rock dropped away. It was practically a straight shot down, maybe two hundred metres or more.

He gazed out over the valley. To the west were the rolling foothills of the Kootenays. To the south were the peaks of the Cascades, across the border in Washington State. Behind him, to the east, were the jagged snow-capped monsters of the Rockies.

Cam settled himself on the edge of the cliff, letting his legs dangle. He reached for his backpack and pulled out two protein bars. He munched them happily, watching the sun drop. Now it was just kissing the mountain peak to the west.

He sat quietly, absorbing the peace and tranquility of the mountain. But soon, the breeze blowing through his damp hair began to feel cold, and his wet shirt clinging to his back made him shiver. It was time to get going.

He took note of the slight quiver in his legs as he walked back to his bike. He knew it meant he was going to be a hurtin' pup tomorrow. Road buzz was also doing a number on his hands; he could barely feel his fingertips. He fumbled badly with the strap buckle as he fastened his helmet.

As he got into the saddle, Cam's heart galloped in his chest. He was seriously stoked for this, his first downhill in—*whoa!* Could it really be five months? He stood on the pedals and did a quick double-check of his brakes. All in order.

Then Cam took a deep breath and pushed off, plunging over the lip into the shadowed dark of the trail.

5

The moment Cam had released his brakes, his bike had jumped away from him like an unbroken horse. It leaped and bucked and twisted under him, at the very edge of control.

As he hurtled down the mountain, the bike's tooth-rattling vibration turned Cam into a mindless jackhammer. He sensed obstacles more than he saw them—branches rushing by like whips, moss-covered deadfall, mucky puddles with oily surfaces swarming with mayflies. Every decision—when to turn, when to skid, when to jump—had to be made in a split second.

At the heart of it, though, Cam knew making it down the hill in one piece was mostly about hanging on. It took guts, more than skill, to keep your hands from flying off the handlebars in unwitting surrender. Guts—and fingers clenched so tight they went into spasm.

Ahead of Cam, a half-dead tree slanted sharply across the trail.

Cam turtled his head, but the obstacle rushed toward him, a lot lower than he'd thought. No way he was going to get under it clean.

He threw the bike into a skid, angling it and his body hard to the left so he'd be low enough to clear.

The expected *thwack!* never came. Cam had made it!

No time to savour it, though. The bike was skidding wildly and heading straight for a knee-high stump.

Cam yanked back with all his might on the handlebars. The bike jerked; he pulled it back where it belonged, up and under him.

For a brief moment, Cam felt like he was totally in control. *Nice...*

But then the bike wheels stalled in the mud, whirring uselessly.

Cam felt himself pitch forward, head-first over the handlebars. His shoulders wrenched in their sockets. His palms burned, then went dead, like they'd been smacked by an electrified ruler.

One numbed hand flew off the squishy grip. It swung wildly, like a rodeo cowboy's on a bucking bronco. Somehow, Cam managed to stay on the bike. Pulling up on the pedals with his toes, he used all his strength to yank the bike out of the mud.

The bike slammed back down to earth beside the tree stump. He tightened up his position over the saddle, then bunny-hopped again, bringing the bike smack down where he wanted it—dead center of the trail and with the wheels perfectly aligned.

Yeah! He was *good* at this! He *had* what it takes—lots of nerve, lots of willpower.

Or maybe he just had, as Dakota liked to call it, "'tude up the yin-yang."

The trail's first real jump was now just ahead. Cam took it at top speed.

"*Woo-hoo!*" Cam shouted as his wheels slammed down on the

far side, an instinctive reaction to the thrill of flight, of easy victory.

He was still riding that wave of elation when the next jump loomed into view. He'd forgotten Dakota had put the two so close together.

He took a deep breath and kicked it, willing the bike up, higher, higher, willing it to clear the jump.

He was over! But his front wheel wobbled as it struck the ground and something deep in his elbow went *ping!*

There was no time for Cam to recover—he was already tearing down a steep straightaway. He remembered that if you didn't nail the sharp curve at the bottom, you'd wind up taking a header into a thicket of something really rude. Something with thorns.

Cam knew instinctively he was moving too fast to make the turn. He had to slow it down.

He applied just a feather touch to the brakes—just enough pressure to take his speed down a click, maybe slow him down enough so he wouldn't wind up with prickles in his ass.

Not gentle enough.

His front wheel jammed itself into the soft ground. His back wheel slewed left, then right, then left again, leaving Cam with zero control as the trail plunged him headlong into a twisty, slippery chute of rock and slime. On the far side of it, the trail was bordered by nothing but air.

Cam slammed on the brakes. He felt them *whirr* against his wheels uselessly. Slick, coated with mud. His rear wheel slid out behind him, heading for the cliff edge.

Time to BAIL!

Cam dove to his left. His elbows crashed first. Then his left shoulder and chin. He was already tucking and rolling when the sharp tug on his leg laid him flat.

His bike shoe hadn't come unclipped from the pedal—and the bike was still hurtling down the hill!

"*Nooo!*" Cam yelled, as gravity and his *fricking* bike and his *fricking useless* shoe dragged him closer and closer *and closer* to the cliff.

Cam flung his free leg wide, hoping to brace himself and stop his fall. But the motion only cartwheeled him around. He grabbed at whatever he could to stop his slide, but none of it made a difference. Not the pine saplings that uprooted themselves and left him clutching stem, needles, and dirt-clogged roots. Not the slippery young shoots that greened the slope and slid through his fists like corn silk.

The bike was going over, and Cam was going with it.

6

t hurt. *He* hurt.

Everywhere.

Impossible to tell where the ache was coming from, though—not unless he moved.

Something told him that was going to be a seriously bad idea.

Cam shifted his weight. An arc of agony slashed his body.

Jesus! What the heck had happened to him?

Cam remembered jack-knifing off the front of his bike. He remembered his foot jamming in the pedal.

The sickening drop…

Then, nothing.

The good news was he had landed…somewhere. And he was still alive.

Barely, he thought.

He tried to open one eye, and another *zut* of pain knifed him in two.

Jesus Murphy!

Lying absolutely still, Cam took a mental inventory of his body. There was blood in his mouth. The taste of old metal made him want to hurl. He tentatively ran his tongue over his teeth. They hurt, but seemed to be all there, more or less. One of the top ones was wiggly.

No brain matter seemed to be oozing from his ears, though, so that was good. The pain in his head was focused on a hard bright knot above his right eye. Probably later there'd be a goose egg there the size of frigging Uzbekistan.

His arms, at least, seemed to be OK when he flexed them.

Then Cam wiggled his toes. There was nothing but air under them. His feet were hanging off the edge of the cliff.

Pure terror pumped through his veins.

Don't move don't move don't move, Cam told himself, *Just open your eyes. Get your bearings.*

He forced open one sticky eyelid. There was green ahead of him—green and grey and brown.

Solid ground.

Safety.

He lunged forward, scrambling and clawing himself toward that green safety net, away from the cliff edge.

Man, that had been close. Too close.

He lay still, letting the panic drain itself from his body. Eventually, the thundering bass line of his heart faded to a steady thrum.

Blinking, he scanned his surroundings. There was just enough light for Cam to take stock.

To take in just how lucky he'd been. *Un-freaking-believably lucky.*

His cliff-dive had been interrupted just a few meters down by an outcrop of grey rock jutting from the side of the mountain like a stony zit. Just a few feet in any other direction and he would have been hurled into the abyss. Even if Cam hadn't been killed outright, a longer fall would certainly have turned half of his bones to chop suey. As it was, he felt like he was a mismatched jigsaw puzzle, with every jammed-together-wrong piece screaming in agony.

So how far had he actually fallen?

Cam ratcheted his neck, notch by painful notch, to look up. Something silvery shone way above his head, catching the last rays of the setting sun.

What the—!

It was his bike, swaying in the air, about three meters up!

Cam pieced together what must have happened. The bike must have snagged in some brush as it went over. The abrupt stop then would have jerked Cam's foot free from the pedal clip. That's how he'd ended up here, instead of dangling by one leg in mid-air with the bike. Or worse.

He suppressed a shudder. It had been *way* too close a call.

He clamped the thought down. There'd be time for him to freak out about it later—but not now.

Now he'd have to hop to it. The dying sun was casting its sharp, red light across the valley. Not much time to get down the mountain before full dark.

Cam tried to get to his feet. Five thousand volts of pure brain-fry coursed through his body.

He sank back to the ground and reached for his left ankle, poking and prodding the throbbing flesh tentatively with his fingertips.

No bones jutting out. No hot spots of agony. Not broken, then. Just sprained.

Even so, it hurt like a bugger. No way he could put his full weight on it. It was going to be tricky climbing back up to his bike, then hauling it back from the brink with one bum ankle.

Luckily, he hadn't lost his backpack when he crashed. There were some first aid supplies in it. He could use them to tape up his ankle. Then, even one-footed, he could coast his bike down the trail, maybe catch a break and flag down a lift at the bottom.

If only he had a cellphone, he'd be able to use it to call for help. But of course his dad thought "a kid" didn't need a phone.

Don't go there, dude, Cam told himself. *Focus.*

"OK, cowboy," Cam said out loud to chase the looming black cloud of panic from his mind. "Time's a-wasting, and there's no time like the present. Up we go."

It was just about the worst thing he'd ever had to do. His bones crunched with every movement, no matter how miniscule. His head swam. Black stars danced in front of his eyes, and the pounding in his ears sounded like a barrelling freight train.

He kept going. Didn't let himself pass out, though Lord knows he was close more than once.

One bloody fingertip at a time, Cam hauled himself up to the top of the cliff.

7

As Cam caught his breath at the top, he let his mind finally run free.

Yeah, his ankle was sprained. And yeah, he was sporting a giant lump above his eyebrow—the kids at school would have a field day when they got a load of that. But otherwise, he was basically in one piece.

A frigging miracle.

But his bike...That was another story altogether.

Lord, his poor bike was a mess. The front wheel rim was twisted beyond repair. It wasn't going anywhere, let alone taking him on an easy ride back to town. Cam was going to have to hoof it.

Great. Just freaking great.

What he needed was a crutch. Cam scanned the brush for something that might do the trick. In the deepening twilight, he could just make out a piece of dead fall that looked long enough to prop up under his arm. He took a few hops toward it, but caught his toe on a snag and almost fell flat. Cam swore under his breath. All he needed now was to sprain the other ankle.

Although it hurt his pride to do it, he dropped to all fours. He scrambled through the brush, looking for the makings of his crutch, swearing as loudly and creatively as he could. It didn't help him find the right kind of stick any faster, but it sure made him feel better. Like whistling in the dark.

He was making so much noise that at first he didn't register the commotion in the distance.

Smash!

Footsteps.

Someone was—*snap!*—chaotically forging his way—*stomp!*—toward Cam through the underbrush!

A wave of relief washed over Cam.

He was just about to call out for some help when a second wave, this time of panic, crashed into him.

The noises were not another hiker or biker: They were the lumberings and crashings of a *very* pissed-off bear.

8

Cam froze in place.

Of course he always knew that bears lived in these mountains. Bears *and* cougars. But shoot—they stayed far away from people if they could, and he stayed far away from them too. He'd never come across one before. Ever.

He scanned the brush, moving nothing but his eyeballs, looking for a shape that wasn't part of a bush or tree.

The snapping and crashing were coming closer and closer.

There! Something.

About ten metres off to his right, a dark blob swelled from the branch of a tree. It wasn't much. It didn't look like a clump of leaves or an abandoned nest. It looked like—

Dammit.

A cub.

It made a chuffing sound.

The cub's mother, somewhere off to his left, answered with a grunting and snuffling of her own. The sound made every hair on Cam's body stand on end.

Now Cam could smell it—her—the bear. A musky odour that made him want to retch. She was coming closer.

And he was smack in between her and the cub. On a direct path to Deceased.

Now what? Now freaking *what?*

His mind spun frantically. Should he hunker down, or try to get to deeper cover? Would the bear see him in the twilight? Would she *smell* him, the way he smelled her?

Instinct took over. As if launched by a spring, Cam flung himself into the undergrowth. Then he rolled onto his back and played dead.

Dear God, he prayed, *please let the bear ignore me. Please let the bear just go collect her baby without a second thought for poor me, or else I'm a dead man.*

The bear was so close he could hear its paws dragging across the ground. He could practically feel its breath ruffling the air around him.

Cam squeezed his eyes shut, held his breath, and prayed.

The cub's grunts grew stronger and more frantic as its mother approached. Cam could hear branches crunching and leaves rustling, closer and closer to where he was hiding...

The mother bear passed right by, so close he could have reached out and stroked her right flank if he'd had a death wish.

He heard the mother's gentle woofing as she scooped the babe onto her back and headed off into the trees, back the way she had come.

At last, the mountain was silent. Cam rolled onto his side, letting his tears of pure relief fall like fat raindrops into the cold dirt.

OK, so he was "safe." From ursine dismemberment, maybe. But not from all the other dangers the mountain could dish up to a guy, alone, at night.

Cam knew that even if the bear had taken off for good—and there was no guarantee of that—he was still in some serious trouble. There was no way he was getting down the mountain tonight. Not in the dark. Not with an ankle the size of a beehive.

Even in mid-summer, the nights got cold up here. There were always stories about idiot, unprepared campers buying it thanks to hypothermia, even in July. Making a shelter was therefore job number one. A shelter and a fire.

It was almost fully dark, but Cam's eyes had adjusted to the half-light. There was still enough to let him check out his immediate surroundings. The good news was that there was lots of cover overhead. And lots of loose material he could use for insulation. What he needed most, though, was something solid to serve as a frame for his shelter. With limited mobility, he wasn't able to build something sturdy enough completely from scratch.

His glance fell upon a sharply angled tree. It stood out against the navy sky like an arrow pointing toward heaven.

Cam scooched toward it on his bum. It was farther away than he thought, which was both a good and a bad thing. Bad, because he was winded and his hands were scraped raw when he got to the tree's base. Good, because its huge size meant its exposed root-ball was almost three metres across, and there was a deep, enclosed space beneath it, large enough for Cam to slip into comfortably.

He grabbed some loose rocks and tossed them into the darkness under the roots. After the *chunk!* he listened for the rustling that would indicate somebody was home.

Nothing. Looking good.

Getting to his knees, Cam foraged about for as many long sticks as he could find. These he propped up around the edge of the root-ball, wedging them into place so they made a solid frame around its free edge. He added sticks crosswise to the frame, fitting them into notches and branches to form a lattice. These, in turn, he covered with leafier branches, piled thickly so the layers would serve as insulation. He remembered the instructor in his survival skills class, the one that was mandatory at Grand Forks High, shouting, "A metre thick! Trust me! You'll need it!"

But *damn!* It was a lot harder to build a shelter on your knees than it was when you were goofing around and mimicking the theme from *Survivor* with your buddies. Just dragging the branches from *there* to *here* was killer.

9

The finishing touches were finally in place.

Cam could barely see his fingers in front of his face—it was full dark. Now it was time to get cracking on his fire. He was stiffening up, though, and every muscle in his body ached. He'd better get a move on before he couldn't move at all.

Cam had never been ace at making fires: they always went out, or choked everyone with nasty streamers of smoke. Nasty and smoky or not, he'd better get this baby going and fast. He'd need it for the heat, certainly. But it was also key for keeping away animals. He thought of mama bear and baby bear, and shuddered—no way he'd want to come face to face with them again.

Cam found some large rocks and set them in a ring near what was going to be the "door" of his shelter. He placed a few flatter ones in the centre as a base. All he needed was to set his own damn shelter—or the entire fricking woods—on fire! He knew that was unlikely, though. Everything up here was soaked from the spring rains, and the ground was cold and damp from snowmelt. He'd be lucky if he could get any fire going at all.

He scooped some fallen pine needles into a small pile. They were soggy—too wet for kindling. He'd have to get ones that hadn't touched the ground—dead ones that were still hanging on the trees.

That was easier said than done with a bad ankle. There weren't that many needles he could reach while sitting on his butt.

Grimacing, Cam struggled to his feet. He hauled himself along, hopping, clinging to the branches of each tree he passed to keep him upright. Finally, he came to a cluster of pines that was still bedecked with last season's reject needles. They reminded Cam of old Christmas trees put out for the garbage truck, their depressing last shreds of tinsel waving in the breeze.

He stripped the dry needles from the branch tips with his free hand, then carefully ladled them into his shirt pocket for the long clumsy crawl back to his shelter.

When he piled them into his fire ring, the needles seemed pathetically few. Hardly worth the effort he'd made to collect them.

He flicked his thumb across the wheel of his butane lighter. Its sharp flare of light came as pure relief. He'd been working blind, really, for longer than he'd realized.

It took several attempts before the fire caught. Cam hurriedly scraped some more needles into it. He was going to have to tend this thing slowly and carefully if he planned to have any hope of making something other than smoke.

The butane in his lighter wouldn't last forever, after all. What if he couldn't keep the fire going, and the lighter failed to produce a flame on the next restart?

Don't think about it, Cam chided himself, willing his nerves to take a break and relax. *Do or do not,* he thought, *there is no try.*

Great—now he was channelling frigging Yoda.

Of course if he had a Jedi lightsaber, he wouldn't have to worry about his stupid, cheap, no-good lighter or his lousy fire-making skills. He'd just *ssssttttt!* and turn the whole forest into kindling.

But he had no lightsaber, no secret Yoda wisdom. Just his own sorry self and his own lousy bushcraft skills. If only he'd paid more attention in that wilderness survival class!

But there was one thing Cam had in spades—pigheadedness. Hadn't his dad told him so a few thousand times?

Well, Dad was a hundred percent right about that. He'd be damned if he let himself give up, especially before he'd even made a full and honest effort at getting this fire going. So Cam kept plugging away.

He crawled on his knees from one end of his poor excuse of a camp to the other. He gathered up whatever debris he could to line the floor of his shelter, plus dead leaves and twigs; really, anything halfway dry enough to feed to his fire.

It was tough going. Removing even the dead branches from the lowest parts of the evergreens was hard; although they snapped pretty easily, he couldn't get any leverage from down on the ground. The effort made him sweat like a pig.

Cam knew the branches needed to be prepped if they were to burn well. Using his pocket knife, he began feathering the sticks so they'd burn better. He worked at one stupid branch for nearly ten minutes, and wound up with just three limp, squiggly curls flaring from the stick's base for his efforts.

Finally, he laid his precious work on the fire.

Nothing happened. It just sputtered out.

10

He hurled himself toward the failed fire and frantically blew on the embers to bring them back to life. Nothing.

One steady blow. Then another. Then another. Cam was growing lightheaded with the effort. His vision started to swim.

Finally the embers brightened. Cam scooped a small handful of leaf litter onto them. But it wasn't dry enough. A spiteful puff of smoke stung Cam's eyes.

Cam swore violently. He was *not* going to let this sucker of a fire die out!

He spilled the last of the yellowed needles from his pocket and slid them into the gasping remains of the fire. They caught!

The flames were tiny, but the embers beneath them grew brighter. With renewed energy, Cam blew on his little hearth fire to keep the glow alive.

This time, as he fed the flames, he made sure to use smaller, more delicate helpings of leaves. *Feed it, don't smother it,* he told himself. *Be patient.*

Not his best quality, that was for sure.

The fire held.

Slowly, slowly, he sprinkled on a few more leaves, then a few more, and a few more. After what seemed like eons, the fire was going steadily, and Cam was finally able to rest on his elbows and allow himself a deep, ragged sigh of relief.

His muscles ached. He felt sweaty and sticky all over. If only he had some more water on him—there was still about half a litre in his Camelbak. He didn't want to use it to wash off, even though the grime on him was making him itch. He'd better save the water to drink later on.

The stickiness all over Cam's hands was what bugged him the most. Resin from the pine branches. He rubbed his palms together, trying to roll as much of the gunk off as he could. Not much came away, but it was better than nothing. He brushed the stuff into the fire.

The small, bright *whoosh* caught Cam by surprise.

What the—? Damn! He'd forgotten!

That bushcraft instructor had made a point of telling the class about pine resin. "Since you guys live in a boreal forest," he'd said, "you might want to remember this."

Resin was highly flammable, he'd told them. And it burnt *even when it was wet.*

Cam couldn't believe what a moron he'd been for the last couple of hours! Wasting so much time building his stupid fire, when he had freaking high-grade fire starter literally all around him!

Cam elbowed his way out of his shelter, then walked on his knees toward the nearest large tree—a whitebark pine. He searched with his fingertips for the telltale crusty white drips where sap had oozed out.

There were lots.

As he pried the chunks of crystallized resin from the trunk, Cam began to relax a little. If he threw a few of them in the fire, he'd be set—it would burn hot enough and long enough to let some of the damp hardwoods he'd collected dry out enough to catch fire. The cottonwood, he knew, would last a lot longer than pine and spruce. And if he ran out of resin, well, there was plenty more just a few crawls away.

Cam freed the first chunk of pine sap from the trunk and dropped it into his pocket. He immediately began working on another as he planned his next task: making a "floor" for his shelter.

Although he clearly hadn't been entirely with it during that bushcraft class, he *did* remember a thing or two. Like that he'd be better off tonight if he wasn't lying on bare ground. Without the sun to warm it, the temperature there could touch down below zero. And frostbite sucked.

So even though Cam's shoulders ached with the effort, he threw his weight into gathering as many low branches as he could, yanking free armload after armload of the flexy pine fronds. Then he shoved them, one after another, into his shelter. The branches would work like a box spring, holding him off the cold ground and acting as a frame for whatever other soft stuff he fill it with for insulation.

The crawlspace inside his rooty shelter was tiny—hardly bigger than his own body—but it still was a massive job to line its floor with branches. *How many would it take anyway?* It seemed like an endless number. The shelter just seemed to swallow them up.

Cam was beginning to shake with fatigue. His whole body ached and his head hurt badly. *And* he was hungry—no, *ravenous*.

Protein bars only did you for so long. What he'd give for a Papa Burger about now...

Ah, screw it.

Cam shoved his last armload of branches into place on the floor of his shelter. He allowed himself to lean into them for a moment. The "bed" wasn't exactly comfy...but not awful either. He might make it to morning without too many cricks in his back or neck.

The shelter sorta smelled nice too. Well, as long as you ignored the choking stink of wet wood. It smelled pine-y, a bit like Christmas.

Cam cut that thought off before it could really take root. Last thing he needed now was visions of sugar plums dancing in his head. Sugar plums, sugar pie, sugar cookies...

Instead, Cam catalogued his good fortune:

His shelter was solid. Bushcraft guy would have to give him an A on it.

And thanks to the resin, he had a fighting chance of keeping a fire going through the night. He'd be unlikely to freeze to death.

That was really all that mattered, after all. He only had to stay alive one stinking night. Once the sun came up, he'd get down the mountain, one way or another. By then, people would be looking for him anyway.

His only job now was to hunker down and wait 'til morning.

11

He hadn't meant to fall asleep. Hadn't even known he *was* asleep until suddenly he wasn't.

But something had jerked him into red alertness. All senses primed, raring to go.

No clue what had done it, though.

Cam lay still in his pine-bough bed, ears straining. Everything was quiet. Serene. Even the yap-happy tree frogs had finally shut the eff up and passed out.

So what had woken him? Was the bear back? Or a mountain lion? He didn't think wolves came up this high, but you never knew...

Cam heard the sound again. The one that had startled him awake.

It was the low rumble of voices. Too far away to tell how many, or what they were saying, but their tone put Cam's teeth on edge.

He knew angry when he heard it.

He knew dangerous.

This was no redneck camping par-*tay* crashing around drunkenly in the woods. These people were trouble with a capital F.U.

The pissed-off voices grew louder. They were coming closer.

Cam listened hard, trying to piece together who the interlopers were, what they were doing here, what they were saying to each other. Although they were still too far away for Cam to make out any words, his gut was getting the gist anyway. And it was warning him, too.

Lay low, brother.

A girl's voice pierced the night.

Shrill. *Scared.*

He couldn't understand her words, but he sensed their meaning: *Don't touch me!*

Cam heard the sound of something solid hitting flesh.

A sharp, short gasp of pain. *The girl.*

Deep, mocking laughter.

Muffled sobs.

Then nothing.

Cam's guts twisted and heaved. Every instinct in his body told him to get the hell out of there and fast. He fought the impulse, though—Cam knew that, as with the bear, his safest bet was to stay quiet and out of sight.

He shifted himself ever so slightly towards his fire. Couldn't put it out completely, or it would send up a torrent of smoke—he might as well blare a trumpet.

Sweeping his hand silently across the bare ground, he banked the fire with some dirt. The fire's sparkling orange eyes dimmed, darkened. Its meagre smoke sat above it, like a fat hen on a clutch of eggs.

Better. The smell wouldn't carry far now, not in the still night air.

At least that's what Cam hoped, anyway.

Peering out through the gaps in his shelter, Cam struggled to catch a glimpse of his unwanted guests. It was hard to pinpoint exactly where they were—sounds carried freakily long distances up here, bouncing off the mountains.

He thought he saw a quick flash of light. There, then gone.

He rubbed his eyes. Could have been nothing. Ghosts in the machine.

Wait—there it was again. A light. Bobbing this way and that. A flashlight.

Cam could hear footsteps now. Shuffling footsteps. Dragging footsteps. *Sad* footsteps. Made him think about a ghost army he once read about in a book.

How many people were there? And why the hell were they tramping through the mountains in the middle of the night?

"I smell smoke," Cam heard. The words now clear as a bell. Coming from maybe twenty meters away—the puny distance from the blue line to the goal. *Too close for comfort.*

Instinctively, Cam scooted backwards, feeling his way like a spider. He knew he had to put some distance between himself and his campfire.

He listened with his whole body as he crab-walked silently into the cover of the brush.

"You and your damn nose," Cam heard someone say. That voice had steel in it. And an accent Cam hadn't heard much around white-bread Grand Forks. "You'd think you were a drug dog at the airport, the things you smell."

"I know what I smell, Jay. Fire. Clear as day," the first man replied. Sullen.

"Give yourself two points, Kav," accent-man replied. "So some trailer-park boys had a cookout here this afternoon. Why should we care? Just keep them moving. We don't have all night."

"Actually, we do have all night," said a third man. His voice was also strongly accented. And reedy, an oboe with a broken mouthpiece. His laughter was sharp.

"Well, I don't plan on being up here all night, Sandip. Nor do our guests, eh?" said the second voice. Cam suspected he was the ringleader. "Do you, sweetheart?"

The girl cried out again.

"Move," Jay said. "Now."

The flashlight's beam seemed less fitful. It was coming closer. Through the low branches of the pines, Cam could now see it was coming from a big-ass light in the hands of a heavy-set, lumbering man. Sandip? Kav? Cam couldn't tell.

The man, whoever he was, was sweeping his torch back and forth so that the people in front of him—maybe four or five in total—could see where they were going. At the front of the line, one of the other men was blazing the trail with a smaller, brighter LED light.

Watching them, Cam's blood ran cold. He realized exactly who these people were. He'd heard the tales—everybody had.

Smugglers had used to choose routes where the terrain was easier, further west near Osoyoos. Flat as a fricking pancake there. But since 9/11…of course the border had tightened. All that B.S. about the terrorists having slipped into America through Canada. *As if.*

The result was the same, though: human traffickers couldn't

use the flatter, easier crossings anymore. They were forced to cut trails through the mountains to smuggle people across the border. These mountains.

The mountain routes were tougher, for sure. But they were also tougher for the border cops to patrol.

Cam swore a blue streak inside his head. Of all the freaking bad luck! What were the chances he'd have landed himself on the smugglers' route? About the same as finding himself on a mama bear's rampage, he figured. And he'd already been there, done that. Obviously, his karma was seriously screwed up these days.

Cam silently moved away from his fire, but he kept his eye on the string of people as they picked their way through the shadows. If he'd been playing "would you rather..." Cam would have plunked for the bear over crossing paths with human traffickers. He'd seen *Kill Bill* on DVD. Knew there was nothing meaner than a guy with a gun and a don't-be-late appointment with a stash of unmarked bills.

So Cam kept moving, inching away from the traffickers. One scootch. Then another. And another. Willing himself to stay calm, keep quiet, not get caught.

Inch by inch, Cam pushed himself deeper into the underbrush. He scootched until he couldn't smell anything but cold night air—not even a whiff of smoke. He scootched until the frightening voices had long faded into the distance. And even then he kept going, one scootch back for every step forward the traffickers took, until the bobbing flashlight beams had disappeared for good over the crest of the hill, and Cam was utterly, completely spent.

12

Cam took stock.

No shelter.

No fire.

And *shit*! No backpack! He'd left it back at his camp.

But going back wasn't an option. Every instinct in Cam's body was screaming, "Get the hell off this mountain—now!" After all, if there was one group of smugglers on the mountain, there might be others. Dollars to doughnuts there were several related gangs all pushing to get through on similar routes tonight.

And human smugglers weren't the only smugglers to worry about. Sure, it was probably too early in the year for most of the drug runners. September was high season for them—everyone knew that. But still.

Cam made his decision. He was heading down the mountain. Now.

But which way?

Doesn't matter—as long as it was the opposite direction from the smugglers.

When Cam tried to stand, though, the ground rushed up at him like a logging truck without brakes. He caught himself with his forearms, saved himself from eating dirt and pine needles, but just barely.

Why the hell was he so dizzy all of a sudden?

He shook his head like a wet dog, trying to clear away the spins. It only sorta worked.

Cam had been kidding himself. He was hungry, weak, and dizzy. His ankle couldn't hold up an ant either.

There was no way he was getting down this mountain before morning.

Cam let his body roll over onto his side. He scooped some moist pine needles under his head like a pillow, and curled himself into a ball. Anxiety wrapped itself around him like a shroud.

Shivering with cold, and with fatigue, and with what he was afraid might even be the start of a fever, Cam told himself, *Just a few more hours, buddy-boy, that's all. A few more hours.*

13

Cam woke with a taste akin to elk dung in his mouth, the screeching clatter of sparrows overhead, and the pale light of near dawn angling over his right shoulder.

He sat up and blinked a few times. Woozy.

This is sooo *not good,* he thought, trying to shake the fog-webs loose from the inside of his skull. *But hey, I'm alive. Not shot in the head by a dude with a 'dead-men-don't-talk' business plan.*

Yeah, well. Maybe he was alive, but Cam felt like he was half-dead. Man, half of him wished he were. Every part of his body ached—bruised from his fall, stiff from sleeping on the cold hard ground. His skull throbbed like he was standing inside an amp, the woofer cranked to brain-shatter.

Cam craned his neck to get a better look at his ankle. It was still swollen, but not quite as tender to the touch. A scrape along his shin was another story, though. He hadn't really noticed it yesterday. Then, it had looked like just a thin line of red—a country back road.

But today, the line was practically the Trans-Canada Highway.

Oozing in places.

Gross.

There was antibiotic cream in his pack. Better late than never to apply it. Cam patted the ground behind him, searching for his backpack.

Damn! He'd forgotten the pack was still up at his campsite, wherever the hell that was. No matter. He'd be home in a couple of hours. He'd clean his leg up—check that, his whole reeking, aching body—when he got there.

Wobbling, Cam got to his feet. He tested his ankle. Yeah, he could put some weight on it now. Not a lot, but enough to be able to hobble down a trail with the help of a stick. Assuming he could find a trail. Or a stick.

He stood for a moment, the blood pounding in his head. He touched the back of his hand to his forehead—it felt like you could fry bacon on it.

Bloody hell.

Cam took a tentative step. He had to hold his arms out like a newbie on ice skates to keep his balance, but he did it.

He took another. And almost fell on his keester.

He wished a nice, long stick or two would just materialize in his hands. Prop up his pathetic, saggy self. But no, he had to find the damn sticks first, go to them, pick them up…

Just the idea made him queasy. His energy level was below the orange zone, looking back up at E. *Waaay* up.

Without much optimism, Cam scanned the area for deadwood. The ground seemed to buck and roll as he turned his head. Bile rose and filled his mouth.

He swore under his breath, stringing together every single ugly swear word he could think of.

He braced himself. Took a step.

His ankle buckled and Cam pitched face first into the dirt, arms and legs splayed. Still, the spinning continued. The whole world roiled like an angry sea, leaving Cam unable to tell which way was up, which way was down.

And then he realized *he* was rolling, too, not just inside his head but really rolling, his body spiralling down slick mossy rocks, rolling like a kid playing on a hill, only he wasn't playing and he couldn't stop himself. His head banged against a rock and light exploded in front of his eyes. He heard water, and the next thing Cam knew he was *in* it, in a furious, rushing cataract of snowmelt that was heading pell-mell for the valley floor a thousand metres below.

The icy water smacked Cam's senses into 'ON' but it was no use. The rocks were slippery with water and algae. There was nothing for his clutching fingers to grab hold of. He was now being pulled down the mountain, feet first, pummelled by water and rocks, his head flopping like a rag doll's. *Ohgodohgodohgod!* he prayed, his body tossed by the water like a leaf.

The water dipped, sped up, as it funnelled through a gap between two large boulders. Then the thrust of the cataract hurled Cam skyward, flipping him over. As he spun through the air, he glimpsed the whitening sky through the trees.

It's the last dawn I'll ever see, he thought.

14

She was suddenly *there,* standing in his path. Knee-deep in the rushing water. For a split second, he could see the grim set of her mouth, her solid, braced stance. Like a defenseman at the scrimmage line, legs firmly planted, hands outstretched, ready to catch him as he catapulted toward her. He was going to smack into her, knock her down, and take her with him.

He tried to scream, "Get out of the way!" but the cold grip of the water stole his breath.

Then Cam felt the contact—the hard slap of bone against bone—and he was tumbled onto his side, out of the water, wrapped in this strange girl's arms, her wet hair in his mouth.

They rolled together on the bank of the cataract, finally coming to stop on a flat rock carpeted with moss and speckled with lichen. Numbed by cold and shock, they lay pressed together, breathless, still.

The girl's eyes were closed, her head thrown back. Cam, still too shaken to move, simply stared at her. He noted her skin, the color of milky coffee; her jet black hair, half of it still in a messy ponytail down her back, the rest hanging limp and damp around her face.

When he finally found the ability to speak, he said, simply, "Thank you."

She jerked in his arms. Then she hurriedly, awkwardly, began to disentangle herself from him. She pushed him away from her as if his cold skin burned hers.

She'd seemed so brave a moment ago. But now she made Cam think of a white-tailed deer about to bolt. Skittish. Aloof.

The girl began squeezing the water from her hair and her clothes.

Khakis rolled to the knee. A plain black t-shirt. No bra.

She saw him staring at her and turned her back to him, continuing to squeeze out the water.

Cam felt a blush rise on his cheeks. It's not like he was ogling her or anything…but he looked away, too.

"I said thank you," Cam repeated, this time, directing his words at his swollen ankle. "You know, for pulling me from the water like that."

The girl shot a sharp glance at him over her shoulder. A humorous twinkle seemed to dance in her eyes. Cam was sure she was about to crack some kind of joke, but then she quickly lowered her eyes and the flash was gone.

Her reply, when it came, was so soft he could barely hear it. "You're welcome. It was nothing."

He couldn't say why, but those oh-so-polite words bugged him. It made him think of sitting in the principal's office, promising through gritted teeth to be a good boy and not make any trouble. It made him wonder where the flash of spirit he'd glimpsed in her had gone, what she was hiding…

But then he remembered what he'd heard the previous night. And he realized that this girl must have been there, been part of it. Might even have been the one he heard scream.

If that was the case, well…no wonder she wouldn't want to call too much attention to herself. Maybe she was already wishing she'd just let him tumble past so she could blast on outta there.

Yeah, he'd want to get away from those creeps too, if he were her.

But Cam didn't want her to leave *him*.

Cam cleared his throat—it had suddenly gone dry—and said, "I think I heard you last night. Walking up the mountain. With a bunch of other people. Was that…you?"

The girl's eyes darted around nervously. "I don't know what you're talking about." Her voice was accented like Sandip's and Kav's, the vowels rolling in her mouth like marbles.

She got to her feet and started picking her way across the rock. "Stay out of the water from now on, all right?" she offered as her farewell.

But Cam couldn't just let her walk off into the woods like that. No way, not yet. He didn't even know her name.

Cam blurted out the first thing that came into his mind.

"That isn't exactly the CAA's recommended route, eh?" he said. "You won't find your way down so easy on your own."

He winced inwardly. Even to his own ears he sounded stupid, cocky. Not exactly the way to keep some nymph from Middle Earth from disappearing back into the mist.

But miracle of miracles: She paused in her tracks.

"*Seeyayay*?" she said. "I don't know this word."

"I guess you're not from around here. *C. A. A.*," Cam repeated, pronouncing each letter distinctly. "The automobile club." He winced again at how stupid he sounded. Felt even worse when she turned to stare at him like he had six heads.

"*Automobile club?*" she said. The fire he'd briefly glimpsed before was there again, flashing in her eyes. She turned her face to the sky and she spoke rapidly, addressing an unseen presence.

"*We are on a mountaintop and he is talking about automobile clubs!* Lord Ganesh! Please help your lowly servant Samira with this…" She waved her arm limply in Cam's direction.

As she turned, Samira's eyes accidentally met his. Her entreaty to the heavens died on her lips.

Cam felt a lurch deep in his gut—a jolt of connection.

But then her eyes slid away from Cam's, and what he thought he saw was gone. *Presto-chango*, she had stuffed her real self away, like a jack-in-the-box latched back into its can.

She gave him a brittle smile. It left Cam feeling like the ground had fallen away beneath his feet.

Who the heck was this mystery girl? And had she appeared out of nowhere, just to mess with his head?

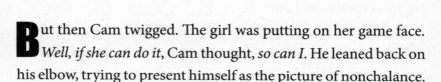

15

But then Cam twigged. The girl was putting on her game face. *Well, if she can do it,* Cam thought, *so can I.* He leaned back on his elbow, trying to present himself as the picture of nonchalance.

"Do you happen to know a better route, then?" she said, her voice controlled and formal. She sat primly, a distance away from him, biting her lip as she scanned the horizon.

"Not exactly," Cam replied. "And with this bum ankle, I wouldn't be much of a tour guide, either." He pointed to his fat foot. "But that's not what matters. Look, I *know* it was you last night. I recognize your voice now. So why don't you just tell me what's going on. I can probably help you. I mean, I've already figured out you're going AWOL over the border…"

She jumped to her feet and started to back away from him, into the bush.

"Please don't go!" he called after her. "I couldn't give two if you're legal or illegal. That's your business. But you were with a bunch of people last night and now you're not. So what happened? Did you get separated? Lost? You don't want to be alone in these mountains. Trust me. I know." He held up his foot.

The girl seemed to deflate before Cam's eyes. She wrapped her arms around her chest, covering herself. Then she sank down beside Cam on the flat rock.

She didn't say anything for a long time. Debating with herself about what to do, Cam figured. She probably knew she'd be in trouble on her own. But on the other hand, why should she trust him? He was just a stupid kid she'd stopped from sliding headlong down a mountain. Not exactly the kind of guy to inspire confidence in anyone.

Cam waited, suppressing the urge to fill the silence with chatter. It was her call, after all. But dammit, he wanted her to stay with him. He *needed* her to stay. No telling how *he'd* get down the mountain without *her*.

When she finally spoke, she just whispered into the curtain of her hair. Her voice was thin, quavery with exhaustion.

"I'm not lost enough. Not at all."

"I get you," Cam said, keeping his voice low and level, the way he spoke to Stargate when the horse was spooked. "Those guys did sound like bad news."

Her only response was to hug herself tighter, trying stop her body from trembling.

Cam propped himself up on his elbow. "So...?" Cam asked gently.

Without looking up, she said, "If they find me, they'll probably kill me. And you, too, if they see you."

She jumped to her feet then, eyes darting like a frightened colt.

Cam put up his hand, palm out. "It's OK. You're OK now. Let's get under some cover. We'll make sure no one will see you. You'll be safe."

"I'm better off alone. You will be, too," she insisted.

60

He swung his legs under him and shakily got up on his knees. "We'll go together. Just give me a second here."

She made a clicking sound with her tongue, turned her back to him, and took a step toward the woods.

Cam reached out, grabbed the cuff of her rolled-up pants leg.

"Don't. Please don't!" he said. "I don't know anything about you, but I do know this: You can't get wherever you're trying to go now alone. No way. You don't know these mountains. I do."

She slapped away his hand but didn't move away from him. He could feel her whole body trembling.

"You may have saved my life," Cam continued. "Now it's my turn to help you. Please let me."

She turned to him, all her earlier diffidence gone. She stared down at him, looking him hard in the eye, sizing him up. Cam could practically see the calculations going on in her head, the complicated algebra of weighing the risks.

"You are pale as death. You're not going anywhere on your own. I will get you a stick to walk with," she said at last. Then she strode off, kicking leaves away as she walked, looking for a crutch.

Cam felt shame sweep through him. *So much for taking control, for* him *helping* her. She'd saved his bacon once. And she was still doing it.

Bloody hell.

He smashed the flat of his hand against the rock, wishing for the thousandth time that he hadn't been such a pigheaded fool. Wishing he hadn't crashed his bike and put himself into this impossible situation. Wishing he was anything, *anyone*, other than Cameron Stewart, The Serious Disappointment.

As he watched her move through the trees, however, Cam felt his spine stiffen. Yeah, he was injured. And he was tired and hungry, too. But he was no weenie. Somehow, he'd make sure to make this thing right. He'd pull it together and make good on his promise to help Samira. No matter what.

When she returned with a tall stick, Cam jammed one end into the ground. With a grunt, he levered himself to his feet. He wavered for a moment, but then he was standing tall and straight, his eyes dead level with hers.

"My name's Cam." He stuck his free hand out, offering to shake hers. She ignored it. "It's nice to meet you, Samira. That's what you said your name is, right?"

She didn't say anything, but he saw the slight dip of her head as she nodded, once.

"And thanks again for saving me," Cam continued. "You're, like, some kickass Lara Croft movie heroine, eh?"

Cam thought he caught a glimpse of a smile playing on her lips before she ducked behind the veil of her hair.

Cam went with it.

"Yeah, you're like, totally bitchin'. Deking the bad guys, plucking flood victims from the rising waters with your pinkie, whisking high-tech ambulatory care devices out of thin air,"—he tipped the stick toward her—"yeah, you're, like, ready for your own movie franchise. 'Samira, Queen of the Cascades.'"

Her laugh was a total surprise. It was loud and full-throated, a laugh that showed all her teeth and made her face light up like the Eastern sky at dawn.

Cam felt an answering warm glow spread in his belly. A goofy grin started spreading across his own face, and he started to sing, off-key: "Samiraaaaaa….Queen of the Cas-CAAAAAAdes!" until he too broke into laughter.

Maybe it was fever talking, maybe it was plain old hysteria. Who the hell knew? But somehow, with this intriguing girl at his side, Cam felt like suddenly everything was OK. Heck, *more than OK*.

Even if human smugglers were after her. *After them both*, Cam corrected himself, if he tossed his lot in with her. But really, what other choice did he have? They were in this together, whether they liked it or not.

The bottom line was that Cam liked it. He liked it just fine.

16

Time to get serious now.

Dropping his voice an octave, Cam said, "OK, let's roll."

She didn't reply. She just stood there, her hands on her hips, waiting for Cam to take the lead. He hop-walked a few steps away from the river. Samira fell into step behind him. They humped along in single file, snaking a path through the thickly set conifers.

Each step was an agony for Cam. His foot throbbed; his head throbbed. He had a new ache in his jaw, too, from clenching his teeth.

A good thing she can't see my face, he thought. He felt like he must have gone the color of spoiled milk. The effort of reaching the cover of the brush had made Cam dizzy again; a cold sweat had broken out across his brow, and had flooded his armpits, too.

God, I hope I don't stink to high heaven.

He glanced back over his shoulder at Samira and saw her grim expression. She didn't have a sprained ankle or a fever, but she was just as baked as he was. Any idiot could see that. Here he'd been worrying that he'd fall over any second. But the truth was, she was about to beat him to it.

He stopped. Wobbled for a second. Wiped the sweat off his forehead with his sleeve.

"We've gone far enough," he said, hoping he didn't sound like too much of a wimp. He scanned their surroundings for a good spot. "There—under that tree. It looks pretty dry, and those needles will be soft."

When Samira didn't reply, Cam manoeuvred himself toward the tree. Although his arm felt like jelly, he held up one drooping spruce bough for Samira to duck under.

Samira sank to the ground. Cam could practically see the strength flowing out of her. She rolled onto her side beneath the sheltering branches and curled herself into a ball. He could hear her murmuring something to herself in her own language—a prayer of thanks?—before she threw her arm over her head and lay motionless.

He sank down beside her.

Her eyelids were closed but they weren't still. Moving like ripples on a lake.

Her lips were slightly parted, and he could hear the soft inhalations and exhalations of her breath, see the gentle rise and fall of her chest.

"When was the last time you slept?" he asked, his voice gentle.

She didn't open her eyes. "I don't know," she mumbled. "It feels like years."

"You'll need to get some, then, if you want to get down the mountain," said Cam. "We can catch a few z's right here."

Her eyes snapped open. Ablaze with black fire.

"We will have plenty time for sleep when we are safe."

"*Whoa!* Just use your head for a second," Cam said. "You're fried. You need to sleep. There's a hard hike ahead, even if we follow a marked trail. But I'm thinking if you want to avoid your boys Skeezer and Cavity, we better not use a trail."

Samira tried to interrupt him, but Cam just kept talking right over her. "Trust me. Rest is the way to go. And this is as good a place as any to do it. They won't find us here. Look around! See? There's nothing to give us away. We won't make any noise. There's no smoke, no fire, no nothing."

She tipped her head, and with one eye, gave Cam a savvy look.

"Sandip was right. He *did* smell smoke. It was from your campfire."

"Scared the crap out of me, too. Got the hell out of there so fast I even forgot to grab my backpack. Talk about stupid."

"Not stupid at all," she said. "They would have killed you if they found you. Trust *me*."

Cam felt queasy. *Time to change the subject.*

"OK. Let's forget about all of that now. Let's just focus on what we gotta do right here, right now. A: You need some sleep or you'll be a zombie in a few hours. And B: To be honest with you, I need some time to let this swelling in my ankle go down some more. And some time to figure out our best route down. So why don't we just chill a bit, catch our breath. We'll both be the better for it if we do. Then we'll make a plan. OK?"

Her answer was just the gentlest, most delicate of snores.

Samira stretched and yawned. "*Hai Ram*," she said.

"Excuse me?" Cam replied.

Samira's cheeks reddened. She sat up and turned away from Cam and smoothed her hair. "Sorry," she said softly. "I wasn't thinking." Her voice had a deep rasp to it, like the buzz of a hornet's nest at twilight. Distinctive.

"What language were you speaking? It didn't sound like English," Cam asked.

"Hindi. It's the language we speak in India. Where I'm from."

"Cool. I never heard anyone speak Hindi before."

She didn't reply.

"Your English is pretty good. For someone from there, I mean," Cam added.

A small sound—a cross between a snort and a sigh—escaped from between her lips.

"What?" Cam said.

"I didn't say anything," she said, a note of alarm in her voice. Like she'd been caught by the principal, cheating on a test.

"No, but you made that sound." Cam tried to imitate it—*sshhhnorf*—"Like you were *thinking* something."

She sneaked a glance at Cam's face, then looked away again.

"Come on. Just tell me. I won't bite, I promise," he said.

She fidgeted a bit. Got a strange look on her face, like she was trying to swallow a nasty piece of gristle.

"We speak Hindi in India," she finally said. There was another long pause. And then her words spilled out, one on top of another, in a rush: "But we *are* a part of the Commonwealth, you know. We speak English, too. At school all day. At home a lot of the time, too."

Now it was Cam's turn to look away, embarrassed.

"Sorry," he said. "I'm a dope. I didn't know."

"It's OK, and now you do," Samira said. An awkward silence hung between them. Cam was relieved when she changed the subject. "How long have I slept?" she asked.

"Not sure. But from the where the sun is, I'm guessing it must be around ten."

"Shouldn't we get going?" she said.

"You feeling any better?" Cam asked. "You looked pretty wrecked when we got here."

"A little." She gave him a wan smile.

"Me, too. The swelling's gone down some, eh?"

He lifted his foot, turning it this way and that to show her his ankle.

Without warning, her face crumpled. And she started to weep.

What the f—!

"Hey. Hey! It's not that bad. Only a sprain!" Cam squeaked. "We'll make it down the mountain, I swear! I can walk on it, see?" He got to his feet and hopped about. "See? Right as rain."

She bowed her head so her hair covered her face. She shook her head.

"It's not that—nothing to do with you. I'm sorry. I'm sorry," she whispered again and again. "I don't normally…not like this, in front of…people." She angled her body away from him, hiding herself even further. Her thin shoulders shook.

"Aw…Samira…" Cam said, crouching by her side. He reached out to touch her shoulder. He let his hand hover for a second, remembering the last time she'd slapped it off. Then dropped it back to his side.

"Please don't cry. It's going to be OK. I promise," Cam said, his voice high and strained. His heart bumped around in his chest. He'd say anything now, promise her the world, if only he could get her to stop crying.

She shook her head again. Between sniffles, she said, "I don't think so."

Cam could see another teardrop fall and splat in the dirt. Confusion ripped through him.

Should he say something? Take her hand and give it a squeeze? Should he put his arm around her? Isn't that what the girls at school did when they had those hallway meltdowns?

But Samira wasn't like the girls at Grand Forks High. So he just sat dumbly, staring blindly at nothing until he heard Samira take a deep, ragged breath and he saw, from the corner of his eye, the shaking of her shoulders lessening.

"Do you want to talk about it?" he asked, as gently as he could. Scared his words might set off another torrent of tears.

But when she spoke, her voice, though still barely more than a whisper, had stopped shaking.

"I do not like to talk about me…my…my personal life," she

said. A pause and then, "I am sorry for…losing control like that. I am very ashamed." Cam saw her head sink even lower toward the ground, and her shoulders bow.

"Nothing to be ashamed of. You've been through a lot," Cam said. Feeling that bump and tumult in his chest again. His mouth as dry as if he'd been chewing chalk.

He shifted his weight restlessly from one haunch to the other. Traced a line with his finger through the spruce needles, took a bunch in his hand. Rubbed them between his fingers until they turned to dust.

"You don't have to tell me anything, Samira. I mean, it's your life. It's just…Well, it might help. People say talking helps. That's what they say, anyway."

She didn't reply.

The silence between them stretched and stretched.

What is she thinking? Cam wondered. *What is she going to do?*

He had no freaking idea. He wished for the thousandth time that she didn't keep hiding herself like that behind the veil of her hair. Not being able to see her face made him feel stranded, at sea, clueless.

Just his luck he'd meet the only girl in Canada who *didn't* want to talk.

18

Then, just as Cam was about to get to his feet and suggest they move on, Samira began to speak. Her voice as tight as an overstretched guitar string.

"My mother died two years ago," she said, speaking to the ground. "My father...it was hard on him. He decided life would be better if we start fresh. Everybody in Mumbai dreams of going to America. So he went.

"I stayed with my Auntie. Only for a few months, they promised me. Until my father gets settled. He will send for me as soon as he gets his green card organized, they said.

"The green card never happened. But my father says it doesn't matter. He is making good money. 'Under the table,' he called it.

"That sounded funny to me, at first. But it isn't funny. It meant when I applied for my tourist visa, the Americans said no. Now we have a real problem. We will never be able to be together again, I think." She took a deep, ragged breath.

"That must have sucked," said Cam. "Why didn't he just come back home to India?"

Samira shrugged her shoulders. "He says there is nothing for us there anymore. And I think he has another reason too. I think maybe he has met someone..."

Cam shook his head. "That figures."

Samira shot a sharp look at him. "No, it does *not* figure. You don't know my father. He is not like…what you are thinking."

Cam held his hands up. "Sorry—didn't mean anything by it. It's just that…well…dads don't always do what they're supposed to, eh? When it comes to looking after their kids."

Samira chewed on her lower lip. "No. I suppose not," she said. "But my father…he is a good father." Her eyes started to well up with tears again.

"So then what happened?" Cam asked quickly.

"Months and months went by. Finally he called. He had a solution. He would send me a ticket from Mumbai to Toronto. I didn't understand at first. I didn't know where Toronto was, that it was not in America."

Cam felt the smile flicker across his lips. *So he didn't know they spoke English in India. But* she *didn't know Toronto wasn't an American city…*

"He said it was all arranged. He had paid someone—a friend of a friend from our neighbourhood—to bring me from Canada to America. And then I understood."

"Snakeheads," Cam said grimly.

"Yes. I've heard them called that, too. People who take you across borders. For money. I knew about people, people from my school, that had gone to America that way. But I never imagined *I* would also go that way, one day. But my father says this is the only way we can be together again. And since I am his daughter I must do what he asks of me."

Cam gave a long, low whistle. "Damn!" He shook his head.

"Your dad sounds like a piece of work. Like my old man."

Samira's eyes flared. "Don't say that! He is a good man, my father. He is trying to do his best."

Cam suppressed a snort. He waved his arm around to take in the mountainside. "You call this 'doing his best' for you? Putting you in the hands of creeps like Sandip?"

Tears rolled down her cheeks. She angrily wiped them away with the back of her hand. "He *was* doing his best. He didn't know…he *couldn't* know."

Cam shrugged his shoulders. "Fine. If that's what you want to think."

Samira rounded on him. "And what do you know about it? You don't know anything about what our lives are like. The choices people like my father have to make every day. You rich Americans with your fancy cars, your fancy clothes. You don't know what it's like to live where millions of people have no roof over their heads, no running water. Knowing that one tiny misfortune is all it would take for you to become one of them."

"Hey—I think you're mixing me up with someone else," Cam said, holding up his hands. "First of all—not American, OK? One hundred percent Canadian, thank you very much. And another thing—"

"Wait," she said. "You're Canadian?"

"Uh, yeaaaah…" said Cam.

"*Na-mum-kin!*" swore Samira, her eyes narrowing. Or at least that's what Cam thought she was doing. Swearing sounds pretty well the same in every language.

Cam's eyes widened in surprise. "That's a first," he said.

"I've never pissed anyone off just by being Canadian. Done it for millions of other reasons, yeah. But not that one."

Samira's cheeks reddened. Then she bit her lip and looked away from Cam. When she spoke again, the fire was gone from both her eyes and her voice.

"I am very sorry. I don't know what I'm saying. I've said much too much. You've been very kind. I'm sorry. It's just that—I thought we were on the U.S. side of border already. But if you are Canadian, that means we are still—"

"Bingo. In Canada."

She wiped the tears from her cheeks.

"So that's that. I never will see my father now."

19

"So how did you wind up here, in British Columbia?" Cam asked when Samira's tears had finally subsided. "We're a long way from Toronto."

Samira took a long, jagged breath. "It happened like this: My father arranged for me to meet a man at the Mumbai airport. He gave me an Indian passport. It had my picture in it but a different name. There was also a visa for Canada with the same fake name."

"I thought you said you couldn't get a visa," Cam said.

"Yes. For America. But it is much easier to get a Canadian visa. Besides, this one was fake, remember?"

Cam blinked. "Right. Duh." He pointed a finger at his temple and cocked his thumb like a gun. Made a sound like a bullet being fired: *pnnnf.*

Samira's forehead crinkled as she watched him. "What is that you are doing?" she asked. Mimicked his hand motion.

"What?" Cam replied. Looked at his own hand, then back at her. He felt a flush of embarrassment. "Nothing. It's like, 'I'm so stupid I should just shoot myself.' It's just a thing we do here." He repeated the gesture. "*Kapow.*"

Her left eyebrow rose slightly. "Hnh. That *is* stupid."

"Yeah. I guess it is," Cam said, feeling like a giant tool. He let his hands drop uselessly to his lap. Then he cleared his throat. "So, go on. You were saying…?"

Samira composed herself, too, before picking up the thread of her story.

"The man told me someone would meet me in the airport on the other end. That person would take the fake papers from me when I arrived and help me with the next part of the journey. When I got to Toronto, everything happened just like the man said it would. When the doors slid open, a woman started waving at me. She ran to me and hugged me like a grandmother. She said I should call her Poppy, like the flower.

"Poppy took me to a tall house, not far from the airport. There were many people there. A few teenage girls like me. A family—a mother who looked very, very tired, with three small children.

"We were given something to eat—something greasy wrapped in paper. I didn't know what it was. I didn't want to eat it, maybe it was beef. One of the other girls said to me in Hindi, 'Don't be idiot. We are all Muslim or Hindu. Poppy, too. They won't give us beef or pork.' So I ate.

"We slept all together in a small bedroom on the top floor of the house. The shades were closed tight tight tight and we were told not to open them, not even peep out under a corner, unless we wanted to get caught and stay in a Canadian jail for the rest of our lives. So no one went near the window.

"Poppy woke us up while it was still dark. She gave us all new travel documents. She said they are plane tickets to *Vangoovir*. I never heard of *Vangoovir*. I wondered if it was closer to New

York than Toronto. I wished I paid more attention to geography in school!"

"She must have meant Vancouver. That's out here. In B.C. The opposite way from New York."

"Yes. I know that now," Samira said softly. "There was a map in the plane." The gentle way she said it made Cam felt like a jerk. Again.

"So then what?" asked Cam brusquely, to cover his embarrassment.

"Jay met us at 'Arrivals.' He scared me. All those horrible tattoos. Skulls. Flames. Monsters up and down both of his arms, around his neck. And his eyes—so cold. He herded us like frightened sheep into a minivan. Sandip and Kavel got on. Kavel told us they are the ones taking us to the United States. We now must do everything exactly as they say. They 'own' us, he said, until we arrive on the other side. Then off we go.

"I was more frightened than ever, but I was so tired. I fell asleep. I do not know for how long. It was early in the morning when we left Vancouver. But the sun was starting to set when the van finally stopped outside a place called Greenwood Motel."

"I know it," said Cam. "Greenwood's not far from here."

"Jay went in a door marked 'office,'" Samira continued. "He came back with three keys. He says half of us will sleep in one room, and he will watch us. The other half will sleep in the second room. Sandip will watch them. Kavel will stay in the third room.

"In the middle of the night, Jay went outside to smoke. I heard Sandip go outside, too. They were talking. In English. They don't think any of us speak it very well. Most of us are from the countryside…"

"But you're a city girl. You speak English at school," said Cam.

"Right," Samira acknowledged. She gave him a tight, thin-lipped smile.

"What were they saying?" Cam asked.

"It was horrible. They were talking about how much money they each would have after they delivered us. How their 'contact' in *Safranisco* was going to pay them 'a premium' when he got a look at us girls—how young we were. How 'innocent.'"

Samira shuddered and clutched herself even tighter. Her voice became high and panicky.

"I knew it had all been a lie, then. That they had deceived my father, my aunt. I knew we would never get to New York. They were kidnapping us! They were going to sell us! To work as—"

She sobbed, unable to spit out the last word.

Prostitutes.

20

Cam put his hand out, lightly touched her shoulder. She tensed, but when she didn't pull away, he reached around and held her to him, offering the only kind of comfort he knew how.

"It's going to be OK," he murmured, unconvinced. Unconvincingly.

Her voice took on a new urgency as the story poured out of her, like a dam had burst and the flood could not be stopped. A huskiness he had not heard before crept in, too. It made her sound strong. Fierce, even.

"I knew I could not let them take me to *Safranisco*. I knew that once we got there, and they gave me to..." She covered her face with her hands. "There would be no way to escape. I decided right then: I will get away from them. But how? Jay was standing guard over us all night. And in the morning, we would begin crossing through the mountains. These mountains."

"So last night then...was that the first chance you had to try to get away?" Cam asked.

Samira nodded. "Yes. I thought about rolling down the car window and calling for help as we drove through that town—"

"Grand Forks. That's where I live," said Cam.

"Yes. Grand Forks. I saw the sign. But Kavel was holding a gun in his lap. I thought he would shoot me if I tried anything.

79

So I stayed quiet. We left the car at the bottom of the mountain. We climbed for a long time. All day. Into the night. They did not let us stop to rest. I thought, 'We will never make it to *Safranisco*, anyway, I will die of exhaustion on this mountain.'"

Cam gave her a wry smile.

"After a while, I told Sandip I have to… go to the toilet. He let me go a little ways away from the group. I walked off into the trees. Then I just kept walking. Trying to keep quiet so they would not hear me going farther and farther away.

"In a few minutes, Jay called out, 'Hurry up!' I didn't answer. I kept walking, faster. I knew he would be starting to look for me right away.

"He shouted to Sandip. All the flashlights clicked on! They were shining everywhere! I ran as fast as I could, without looking back, hoping they were making so much noise they could not hear me. Somehow, they didn't find me. You found me instead," she said.

"If you want to put it that way," Cam said. "But I think *you* found *me*."

"Either way, we are here now. And we are still in Canada." Samira fell silent. Her eyes met Cam's. Locked onto them.

A buzz went through Cam's body. *That feeling of connection again.*

Intense. Unsettling.

"We've got to get you away from those guys for good," Cam said, swallowing hard, keeping his eyes on hers. "The tattoos you described? Those sound like the ones the United Nations gang uses. If Jay and the others are part of that gang, you won't be safe anywhere. Not unless we get you to the authorities."

A small sob escaped from her. "I can't go back with you! If I do, I'll never get to my father…!" She buried her face in her hands.

"Maybe not this time," Cam agreed, regretfully. "But I can't see trying to get you over the border into the States now, just you and me. There's nothing but a zillion directions of wilderness over there. And the U.S. Border patrol. They've got GPS and helicopters and remote sensors and stuff up the yin-yang. They'd pick you up as soon as you stumbled into town. Assuming you made it to a town."

Samira didn't reply. She just rocked silently, back and forth, moving her lips in soundless prayer.

21

Cam's mind was whirring furiously. The U.S. Border Patrol, he figured, was the least of their problems. More worrisome was Jay and the rest of the traffickers. If they crossed paths with them again, there was no telling what could happen. None of the possibilities were good.

Their best option was to get back to Grand Forks without being spotted by anyone. Then, maybe they could figure out another way to get Samira to her dad. And if not? Well, Cam figured getting sent back to India was still a better choice than getting shot in the head by pissed-off gang members.

Cam cleared his throat. "Listen to me, Samira. Jay and Kavelwhateveryoucallhim, they're going to be looking for you. You're worth money to them. So where would they look? Which way would they think you'd try to go? I know if I were them, I'd be thinking you'd head straight down the mountain as fast as you could, back to town. I'd send someone to wait for you on the trail back. To intercept you.

"So here's what *I'm* thinking…We have to outsmart them. Think in a different way. Not go straight back down lickety-split. But take a detour. Go the *opposite way*. Up," he finished.

He leaned back on his elbows, studying Samira for her reaction.

"Up," Samira repeated dully.

"Yes. Up. I think I've got a pretty good idea where we are now—now that my head is clearer. I've been on this part of the mountain before. Lots of times. And if I'm right, there's a most excellent cave not too far from here. Where we can lay low for, let's say, another day or two. Just long enough for Jay and the others to give up. They can't wait forever."

Samira's brow furrowed.

"I don't know…what you say makes sense…but how will we know when it is safe to go to your town?"

"We won't," Cam replied bluntly. "But I'm thinking every hour we delay going back to town brings us an hour closer to safety. Look, you're worth money to them; they won't want to lose you. But the other folks they were bringing over the border—they won't want to risk losing them, either. The longer it takes them to get to San Francisco, the more likely it is that they'll get caught, or someone else will run away, right? So how long will they be willing to stick around and look for you? Like what, one more night? Two, max? It's all about the law of diminishing returns."

"So you're saying we have to stay out here. For another night. In a cave." She shuddered.

"Exactly," Cam said.

Samira weighed the idea over in her mind. "Can't we go a different route—say, to another town?" she asked.

Cam shook his head. "The next closest town along here is Midway, and that's more than fifty clicks away. As the crow flies. We don't have enough gear to do that trek. Even if my ankle was OK, it would take more than a week to get there. *If* we found a

83

passable trail. But if we had to bushwhack it? *Naah.* Forget it. No can do. But we *can* sit tight. The only problem with this plan is food. But I'm thinking I'd rather go hungry for a day than be dead for a lifetime."

"I've got a little food…" Samira reached into one of the pockets on her pants leg and pulled out three foil packets of airplane nuts.

She smiled wanly, but there was that little twinkle in her eye again, the one Cam had glimpsed so briefly, but which had intrigued him so much.

"Bonus!" said Cam, clapping his hands once. "We can feast for a week."

A shadow crossed Samira's face. She closed her eyes for a moment, and a deep vertical crease formed between her eyebrows. She was thinking hard, trying to come up with a better alternative to the plan Cam had proposed.

"No," she said at last, opening her eyes and fixing Cam with her hard black gaze. There was iron in her voice now. "You cannot do this, Cam. Your ankle is *not* getting better. Any idiot can see that cut on your leg has gone bad. You look feverish too."

Cam started to protest, but Samira stopped him cold with a click of her tongue.

"We will do this instead: You will tell me how to get to your cave. I will wait there. Alone. You will go back down without me. Maybe get help…"

"Forget it!" shot back Cam. "There's *no way* I'm going down this stupid mountain without you, Samira. Shit, I don't even know if I *could* with this damn ankle. Besides, I don't like the

84

idea of running into those goons any more than you do."

Their eyes met. Cam felt that almost electric connection again. It practically knocked Cam sideways.

"So, it's settled. We go together. To the cave," he managed to say, although his throat had tightened and his mouth had gone dry. "We'll wait. Twenty-four hours. Together. OK?"

"OK," she agreed, so softly he could barely hear her.

"Onwards and upwards, then," Cam said, struggling to his feet. He felt weak as a newborn puppy. "*Madame*?"

Samira hesitantly took his proffered hand. She turned her face shyly away from his, but then her fingers clasped his own. Tight.

"Onwards and upwards," she echoed.

Onwards and upwards.

22

Cam rooted around for the sturdy limb Samira had found for him. He got to his feet and propped it under his armpit.

The rest really *had* helped. He could put his bad foot down on the ground now—not that it could hold his full weight for long, but he didn't have to hop anymore. He could hobble along at a pretty fair clip where the ground was even. And where it wasn't? Well, Samira wasn't moving much faster than he was, anyway.

His fever had receded somewhat, too. Didn't his mom always say you needed to rest when you were sick? Yeah, well. She was right. He wouldn't say he felt like a million bucks, not by a long shot. But he figured he had enough juice to get them safely to the cave. Then it would be just hunkering down and waiting. Nothing easier than that.

Cheered by his renewed energy and by having a plan, Cam led the way out from under the trees. They headed back to where he and Samira had first crossed paths—the rushing river. At the flat rock where they had both caught their breath, he turned to the left and headed upstream. Side by side, they cautiously picked their way through the jumbled rocks that littered the north-facing bank.

After about ten minutes, they came to a bend in the river.

Above the bend, there was a true waterfall, cascading through a tumble of boulders in a series of steep switchbacks.

Samira sighed. "How do we get up that? Unless you are like Lord Hanuman that can climb up a coconut tree."

To Cam, the words felt like a challenge. Even if she didn't mean them that way. He wanted to show her, prove to her, that he was worth sticking by. Not as her charity project, but because he could help her, too.

"Naah—it's a piece of cake," Cam said.

He grasped his walking stick firmly at one end, hoisted it on his shoulder like a javelin, and heaved it into the air. It disappeared over the top of the waterfall, landing somewhere out of sight with a rustle and a *thunk*.

He began scrambling up the rocks alongside the waterfall. Thankfully, there were lots of handholds, not too far apart; this was nowhere near as hard as the climb up to his bicycle had been.

When he was about halfway up, he heard Samira say irritably, "OK then, fine. No way *I* can get up that. *Aiyee*, I am not a mountain goat."

Cam felt his insides relax. *Victory.*

The good feeling was short-lived, though. It would be a hollow victory if Samira couldn't follow him. He called out, encouraging her, "It's easier than it looks. Just test each hold before you move. You'll be fine."

Cam watched Samira tentatively begin her ascent. He saw her prod each rock before stepping onto it, then grab hold with both hands before she shifted her weight to her other foot at a higher level.

That was good. She was cautious, but not timid.

Reassured, Cam resumed his own climb. The rocks were wet and slippery, but there were plenty of handholds, and everything he touched was stable.

He looked back regularly to check on Samira's progress and was glad to see she was climbing with greater confidence. She was even catching up to him! He'd have to hustle if he didn't want her nipping at his heels, teasing him—

"*Saala Gandu!*" Samira swore. "Making me behave like a monkey!"

Then he heard her strangled gasp. When he glanced back at her, he saw she was hanging, frozen, midway up the rockface.

He knew exactly what had just happened.

"Did I, um, tell you not to look down?" Cam asked.

The small, scared reply floated back to him.

"No."

"Don't look down," he said.

"Too late."

Cam heard more mumbled swearing. Then: "Cam! I'm scared! *Hai Ram!*"

Cam knew how dangerous it could be to panic when you were climbing. It made people make stupid mistakes. "Samira!" he called down to her. "Look at me. Look at me! Now!"

Her heart-shaped face tipped up and her dark terrified eyes met his.

"You're doing great!" Cam declared. "Now all you have to do is keep doing what you're doing. Moving one hand at a time. Then and only then, when you are set, move one foot. That's it.

Easy."

"But—"

"But nothing. Stop talking. Look only where your next move is going to be, and up at me. Got that?"

There was a slight hesitation before she nodded. But then Samira resumed climbing. One hand moving at a time, her eyes alternating between watching her hands and feet and looking up at Cam's face.

23

"**S**ee? That wasn't so bad," Cam said as he reclaimed his alder crutch at the top.

"I suppose not," Samira agreed, without quite as much confidence in her voice. But she forced a smile. "Onward and upwards, eh?"

Cam grinned. He *liked* this girl.

They hiked side by side along a faint remnant of a trail that hugged the top of a ridge. It passed through large, widely spaced trees which eventually gave way to openings and views across the valley.

"It is so beautiful!" Samira breathed.

"Yeah, it is. But let's not waste too much time admiring the view—let's get to that cave ASAP," Cam said.

The trail took them on an up-and-down route over a prominent knoll before descending about a hundred metres and heading back into the forest. There, it crossed a wider trail that headed east-west on an easy grade.

"This is it," crowed Cam triumphantly. "We're only about five minutes from the cave now."

Cam turned left, and began walking as quickly as his bum ankle would let him: in a kind of half-walk, half-hop gait that made him feel like a new bunny.

Samira hustled from behind him to walk at his side. "You spend a lot of time up here, then."

"Whenever I can," Cam said.

"I can see why," Samira said. "It's so...peaceful."

Cam laughed. "Yeah, when you're not being hunted down by scumbags who want to kill you."

"Thank you for reminding me," Samira said. "Although it's not as if I had forgotten. It was just for one small second, I was pretending they didn't exist."

Cam had no answer for that. Felt like a dick for having brought up Kavel and the others.

They walked along the trail until it came to a large clearing. It angled up steeply on the east side.

Samira's face was red and there were beads of sweat along her hairline.

"You OK?" he asked.

"That was more than five minutes," Samira scolded.

"I've never been good with keeping appointments. Guess my inner clock is messed up." He pointed into the distance. "You see up there? Right above where those trees seem to form an upside-down V? That's the entrance to the cave."

Samira squinted, shading her eyes with her hand. "Not really," she admitted.

"That dark blotch. With the sparkly bit beside it? That looks brighter than the rest of the rock? Those are quartz crystals. The cave is lined with 'em. "

"If you say so. I just see rock. And trees. And more rock."

"Doesn't matter," said Cam, vaguely disappointed. "Just

wanted you to know we're almost there."

"Right. Five minutes only," Samira said.

He lippety-lopped ahead. "C'mon then, if you're in such a hurry."

The next part of the trail was steep. Cam and Samira laboured up the hill, panting, until they came to the first of three switchbacks.

Cam paused at the turn, giving Samira a chance to "catch up." The truth was his ankle was throbbing, and a sick, cold sweat was dripping into his eyes, but he didn't want to let Samira see how hard he was working. He sensed that she needed him to be strong, in charge from now on.

How was he going to pull that one *off?*

Not a clue, but he was damn sure going to try.

A creek crossed the trail at an oblique angle. They waded through it but had trouble picking up the trail again on the other side—it had been washed out, and the slope was covered with treacherous scree.

Samira said, "The trail is gone."

"Doesn't matter," said Cam. "I can see the cave. Just stay close behind me. Plant each foot down firmly so you don't slip on the loose stuff."

He struck out, heading uphill along the creek's south bank. The hillside seemed to crumble beneath them at each step, but they gave each other their hands to steady themselves. After about two hundred meters, they reached an area where the creek spread out and flattened. It was littered with jagged white pebbles.

"Quartz," Cam told Samira, pointing to the rocks. "That's

what makes up the crystals in the cave, too. Too bad we don't have a flashlight. The best ones are around this kind of dogleg at the back."

He tapped the lighter in his shirt pocket. "But once we get a fire going, we can make a sort of torch and bring it in there. Yeah, that'll do the trick. They'll look awesome by firelight."

Anxious to get to the cave, he lippety-lopped, lippety-lopped as fast as he could go up the last slope. Waiting at the top for her to reach him, he realized how tired she had to be. She was literally trudging—shoulders hunched, head bowed, eyes to the ground. She was being held together by nothing but grit and willpower and nerves of frayed steel.

Cam felt his heart melting. The urge to protect her, to take care of her, was stronger than anything he had ever felt before. Stronger and more disturbing.

You're on a frigging mountain, boyo. Trying to escape killers, or have you forgotten that little factoid? This is no time to for going all googly. Get over yourself.

He shoved the uncomfortable feelings aside.

When she was at last alongside him, breathing hard but smiling, he swept his arm through the air.

"*Ta dah*," he sang.

The entrance to the cave was gouged halfway up the bare, rocky slope beside him; the rocks surrounding it sparkled in the morning sun.

24

Samira reached out her hand. Fingered the bumpy surface of the rock.

"It's how I always imagined snow would look like," she breathed. "Magical."

Cam laughed out loud. "I suppose it does look like snow, in a way. After it's sat for a while and gone all crusty. And snow does kind of sparkle like that in the sun too, sometimes. Not a lot, but sometimes."

"I'd like to see that," Samira said.

"Well, let's hope you don't get to see any snow just yet. It can still snow up here, even at this time of year. And believe me, it wouldn't be magical trying to get through these mountains in a snowstorm. Without gear."

Samira shuddered. "Are you *trying* to terrify me over and over again, or is that just you being your charming self?"

Cam felt his cheeks suddenly grow red. But then he saw the goofy expression on her face and realized she was just teasing him.

His face grew even hotter.

"Er, let's get inside. Out of sight," Cam mumbled, busying himself wedging the alder crutch into a rock crevice to hide his telltale blush. Didn't want to let her know she'd got to him. Not in that way, anyway.

Cam scampered up the slope and into the coolness of the cave. It smelt musty, in the way that all caves seemed to smell, but good just the same. The smell of good, honest rock.

He heard the scramble of Samira's shoes on the rock. She swore again, using words Cam didn't know. Then her face appeared at the cave opening. He admired the determination in her eyes, in the set of her jaw.

"Let me guess. What you just said was, 'Thank you, my hero Cameron, who has brought me to this haven of safety in the wilderness.'"

Samira grinned. "Not exactly."

"So what *did* you say then?"

"Better you don't know," she said, "or you might not think well of me." She clambered over the lip of the cave and sat beside Cam. "How did you find this place?"

"Some of the guys know it. Come up here in the summer to get high, shoot the shit. You know. Come on. Lemme show you around."

Cam crawled a bit deeper into the cave. Light still penetrated there, so you could see how some stones had been arranged to make a crude seating area around a fire pit. There were some charred remains of sticks in it, making the pit looked like a dead, black eye amid the sparkling whiteness of the crystal walls.

"This is the 'Crystal Palace,'" Cam explained. "Or as my friend liked to call it, 'The Crystal Meth Palace.'" He pointed into the shadows. "Some of the guys like to overnight here. 'Bad-Boy Boy Scouts.' You sleep toward the back. I've even done it once. It's cool. You just bring your sleeping bag and an air mattress, get a fire going in the fire pit to keep animals away, and you're set for the night."

"Practically a five-star hotel," Samira said, picking up on Cam's good spirits.

"You betcha. Here. I'll show you."

He crawled forward slowly, letting his eyes adjust to the diminishing light. Samira followed at his heels. It took just a few moments to reach the point where the cave took a sharp turn to the right—a dog-leg.

The deepest—and thus the safest—part of the cave was around the bend, completely invisible from the outside. But the L was also the most beautiful; the crystals coated practically every surface. Cam remembered how the first time he'd been here, he'd snapped on his flashlight and had been blown away by the dazzling white surrounding him.

But now, without a flashlight, Cam would have to just feel his way toward a spot he remembered—the spot he'd laid his sleeping bag the night he'd been out here with Dakota.

He inched forward.

Samira, however, hung back.

"I can't see," she said. Not a whine. Just a simple declaration of fact.

"It's OK!" Cam replied. "I've been here before. The ground is flat. The ceiling even rises up a little. Just stay behind me and you won't bump your head or anything."

"Do we really have to go so far? No one can see us already, can they?" Samira said.

Cam crept farther into the L.

"I hate not being able to see. Why don't you toss me your lighter, if you want me to follow you?"

He didn't want to. He hated not having his lighter right where he liked it, in his shirt pocket at all times, when out on the trail.

"Come on, Samira. You won't need it. I promise."

"Please?"

Cam sighed. "OK. But don't use it unless you really need to. We can't afford to waste the butane. We need it to light our fire later."

He fished the lighter from his pocket and fumbled in the dark 'til he felt her hand. Then he pressed it into her palm, but didn't let go until he felt her fingers curl and tighten around it. Not even then.

"Thanks," she said. "Just having it makes me feel better. I won't use it. Not unless I really need to."

"OK."

She pulled her hand away from his and Cam resumed inching forward.

"Now, if I remember right," Cam called over his shoulder, "over here to the left is a perfect place to hang. It's smooth, almost like it's been polished. And pretty flat too. Yeah, this is it. You see how the rock just seems to—"

He let out an inadvertent yelp of shock, recoiling as if he'd been stung. Then he sprang back, turned, and pushed Samira as fast as he could back toward the cave mouth.

"What? *What*?" screamed Samira, as they scrambled through the cave at a frantic pace.

When they were safely back outside, Cam said, "There's an animal in there. Don't know what kind." Cam was blowing hard. "Something furry."

"Is that all?" Samira asked. She was sitting on the lip of the cave mouth, her feet dangling. "Gosh, you nearly scared me to death."

"What do you mean, 'Is that all?' I'm telling you, I touched some weird animal. It was freaky."

Samira turned her dangling feet this way and that, like a little kid on a swing.

"Funny," she said. "I didn't hear anything. We had bats in the bathrooms at our school. You always knew they were there; first, because of the smell, and then because they made rustling sounds all of the time. Animals usually make some kind of noise. Unless they are dead. And most animals, not live ones anyway, certainly don't let you *touch* them."

Cam felt like a total jerkwad. "Yeah...You're right. It probably was a dead bat," he said sheepishly. "My hand touched it and I just went...*waaah!* I guess I kind of overreacted."

"Probably," said Samira. "But we do need to check. I mean, if we are going to spend the night here."

Cam stared at her in disbelief. "Doesn't the thought of an animal in there—alive *or* dead—give you the willies?" he asked. "What kind of self-respecting girl are you?"

She shrugged her shoulders. "Where I come from, there are animals everywhere. Birds, bats. Bugs. Especially bugs. And I can tell you I'm less afraid of a dead animal than I am of Kavel and Jay. So," she said, her voice all business. "Shall we check together? Or would you rather I go back in myself to check? I don't mind."

98

Samira's question ripped a nine-inch gash in Cam's pride.

So much for appearing confident and strong...

"No," he declared. "I'll go. You wait here."

He was ten feet into the cave before he remembered he'd given Samira his lighter. *Damn.* Didn't want to look like a total wuss by going back out to ask for it. But he wasn't about to touch anything with his bare hand again, either. Not if he could help it.

Cam spied a length of charred wood in the firepit. It was still solid, only burnt around the edges.

That would do the trick.

He grabbed the stick. With his heart in his mouth, Cam crawled to the back of the cave. He reached the dogleg and turned to his right. Cautiously, he edged forward, letting the stick sweep the ground for obstacles ahead of him.

When it touched the *whatever,* Cam's whole body jumped.

He'd hoped it had skittered away. That he'd just imagined it...

He prodded the thing with his stick.

It didn't move.

Samira was right, then: dead.

Cam poked it again with the stick. The thing was still there, immobile. He swung the stick to the left and to the right, touched "it" in both directions.

Whatever kind of animal it was, it was bigger than a bat.

Reluctantly, Cam kept probing the thing. Its contours started to form in his mind.

Then it dawned on him.

It wasn't a dead *animal.*

What he had touched was human hair.

25

"Well? Is it still there? What is it?" Samira asked, her voice at his ear. She had crawled into the cave behind him, practically on his heels.

Cam didn't want to answer her. Didn't want to admit to himself what he already knew to be true—that there was a dead body lying just inches in front of him! All he wanted to do was turn and run, and keep running, all the way back down the mountain to his own house and his own bed where he could throw the covers over his head and tell himself this had all been a bad dream—and not just any bad dream either, but the biggest, baddest granddaddy of bad dreams ever.

But Samira was blocking his retreat, and there was nothing he could do but try to calm the frantic staccato of his heart, and find some way to tell her what he'd found without his voice squeaking like a girl's.

"Stay back!" he said. "You're right, it's dead. But it's worse than we thought. It's—"

Samira flicked the lighter on and gasped in horror.

There was the body, dried and shrivelled like a mummy. A thick curtain of black bangs caressed sunken, leathery eye sockets.

Samira quickly snuffed the lighter's flame, but the awful

image still blazed in Cam's mind. The boy—and it probably *was* a boy, a teenager like themselves—was curled up, arms wrapped around himself, like he had gone to sleep for the night. Maybe shaking with the cold, trying to hold his thin green jacket closer to him for whatever warmth it could offer.

It was the shoes that got to Cam the most. He knew that for the rest of his life, he'd never forget how those worn, knock-off Adidases had looked, the toes turned in toward each other like a little kid's.

Scuff marks on the toes.

Like the ones on his own Vans.

He could hear Samira starting to cry, and his own eyes filled, too.

Be strong, he told himself. *Be a man.*

Yeah, right.

He could hardly breathe. The still, dank air of the cave was clinging to him like a shroud. A slick sheen of sweat coated every inch of his skin. He was shaking, too, chilled to the bone.

Cam turned his body toward Samira's. She was reaching out for him, and he took her in his arms. They clung to each other for God-only-knew how long, shaking, unable to think or to decide what to do next.

"Come on," Cam managed to squeak, finally. "Let's get out of here. We'll find somewhere else to hide out tonight."

He eased his way around Samira and started crawling back out through the cave, still gripping Samira's hand in his.

"No! Wait!" she replied, pulling him back into her arms. "We can't just…leave him here! Not like that. It isn't right."

Cam sank back on his heels. He took a few deep breaths to try and quell the sense of panic that was rising in him. He simply *had* to get out of that cave.

Still, somehow he forced himself to keep his voice level, calm. "This dude's been here all winter. Maybe longer. Another night won't hurt him. Come on, Samira. Let's go."

In answer, she flicked the lighter on. She held it like a wedge between them.

"We have to do something," she insisted.

"Like what?" Cam asked.

"I don't know...something."

She twisted around and raised the lighter above her head so it cast its glow over the body. Over her shoulder, Cam could see the corpse, looking like he'd just gone to sleep for the night. Seeing him there like that, so vulnerable, filled Cam with the urge to toss a blanket over him, tuck him in, hide his shrivelled body...

The flame flickered, casting macabre shadows over the dead boy. The sight sent shivers through his whole frame. Cam's throat closed. He needed air. Fast.

He was just about to tell Samira to hurry up, to get the hell out of the cave before he upchucked, when she gasped. "No. It can't be..."

"What?" he said, his breath coming in shallow gusts.

"His jacket..." she said softly. "I think I've seen it before..."

"Aw, jeez, Samira! It's a frigging army jacket! A billion people have ones just like it. Come on! Let's get out of here now!"

She ignored him. Her voice was thin, almost spectral.

"I remember a jacket just like it. You see? That patch on the pocket? A boy in my school had one on his…"

She let the lighter go out again, so her next words floated to Cam's ears out of the darkness.

"I think this might be him," Samira whispered, her voice choked with anguish. "Ambar Achari. He was a year, maybe two, ahead of me in school. He went to America last year with his family. Bragging about how rich they were going to be once they were here. No one ever heard what happened to him. All us little fools, with our laughter and jokes and snide comments, saying he must be driving a fancy car and living the high life.

"But he wasn't living the high life—he'd been brought through these same mountains, just like me. And he's been here. Dead! This whole time! And we never even knew."

Cam held her again, for what seemed like ages, as she wept into his shoulder. He stroked her hair and murmured again and again, "It's all right, it's all right."

But things plainly weren't all right. They were anything but.

26

Once they were finally out of that cave, Cam turned his face to the midday sun, wishing the heat and brightness of it would scour away his feelings of revulsion. But it wasn't working. He could still see that guy in his mind's eye—all dried out and leathery. A Tim Burton nightmare of an apple-doll.

No matter how hard Cam stared at the bright sky, at the swaying trees, at the hard, glinting angles of rock and stone, nothing could erase that horrible vision of the mummified body from his mind.

He couldn't figure it out either—how somebody could get like that. Why hadn't the corpse rotted—become a skeleton even? Cam wracked his brains, wished for, like, the zillionth time he'd paid more attention in science class.

Maybe it had to do with the cave—how cold it was, how dark it was, how dry it was in there. Like when you find a hard, shrunken orange that had gotten lost in the back of the fridge. Dehydrated instead of decomposed.

Cam shoved the disgusting thought from his mind. Vowed never to watch *CSI* again. Never to eat oranges again, either.

He shot a quick look over at Samira. She was hunkered down a few feet away from him, her blank eyes fixed on the pebbles at her feet. He couldn't even begin to imagine what she was going through. Hell, this whole thing made him want to puke his guts up, and he didn't even know the guy. She did.

She wasn't crying anymore at least. But this zoning-out thing she was doing now, well, it wasn't much better. What if the shock made her go mental—catatonic or something?

Well, he'd be screwed. He wouldn't be able to leave her. Wouldn't be able to get her down the mountain, either.

He eyed her surreptitiously. He didn't want to push her. Any idiot could tell she needed some time to pull herself together. But they had to do something. It wasn't going to be daylight forever, and if they were going to get to another cave, well, first they'd have to find one.

Cam sure as heck didn't want to spend the night in *this* cave, not with the dead guy.

"Samira?" he said softly.

No answer.

"We really ought to get going. Find someplace else to camp tonight."

No answer.

"Samira? Please? We can't help him by just sitting here."

"We can bury him," she said. "Put his body to rest. So his soul can be freed."

A wave of irritation rippled through Cam. He forced it down.

"I hear you, Samira. I wish we could. But we'd need shovels and shit for that. We'll get someone back up here tomorrow to take care of it—*him*. I promise. But we can't bury him ourselves, not right now anyway. The best thing we can do for him is the

105

same thing we have to do for ourselves: get outta here."

"We can still cover him. With branches. Or…something."

Cam grimaced.

She lifted her face to him, and Cam could see the stubborn set of her jaw.

"What if it were *you* lying there like that? Would you want people just to say, 'Oh, such a shame,' then go toodling off, leaving you there like they had never seen you?"

Cam wanted to yell at her. Just say, "The hell with it—who cares? Let's just get out of here *now*!" But he forced himself to keep it together. To think about what Samira was saying.

Would he want his body to be left like that? No, he wouldn't want that.

He reconsidered what Samira was asking—build some kind of tomb for the kid.

Yeah, they could do that. It would be like when he made the pine-bough bed in his shelter the previous night. Only with a dead guy under it.

He suppressed a shudder.

"OK," he sighed. "We can get some branches from the trees. Make, like, a cover for him. Would that make you feel better?"

Her gaze was steady, warm, when it met his.

"Yes, Cam. It would. Thank you." She got to her feet. "Do you have a knife of some sort I can use to cut the branches?"

Cam reached into his pocket for his Swiss army knife. He started to say, 'Don't worry about it, I'll get the branches,' but Samira stopped him.

"This is something *I* need to do for him. May I?"

She held her hand out, palm up. Cam placed the army knife in it.

She strode off into the bush, and Cam could hear the branches swishing and swaying as she moved through them. Then he heard her grunting with the effort of trying to saw through even the thinnest branches with his lousy two-bit knife.

It was her damn idea. Let her look after it, he thought angrily. He was so tired, after all. Hungry, woozy—miserable, too.

But he couldn't just sit there. Not while she was struggling to do something decent. In his heart of hearts, he knew she was right.

So despite himself, he grabbed his crutch and hobbled into the brush toward where Samira was hacking away at the pine boughs. She glanced over her shoulder at him, but didn't stop sawing the branch she was working on.

Cam gathered up a few of the boughs she had already cut. He wedged them under his free arm and carried them back to the cave entrance. He lifted two branches away from the others. Grasping them with his left hand, he took them with him as he crawled back into the grotto. Kept crawling, all the way into the dogleg, even though every fibre in his body revolted.

He took a deep breath to steady himself. Then he clicked on the lighter. As he held the lighter aloft in his left hand, he used his right to lower the pine boughs over the boy's body.

"Rest in peace," he murmured, feeling utterly foolish.

He adjusted the boughs slightly, so the boy's feet were covered.

There. Now I won't have to see those sneakers again.

107

Samira was waiting for him at the cave entrance. Her face was red from the effort of cutting the wood, and he could see from the streaks on her face that she'd been crying again. But for now, at least, she was dry-eyed.

"I will do the rest," she said. Her voice edged with steel.

"You don't have to—"

"I want to. Thanks, Cam. But please. Let me do this. I have to. For Ambar."

He nodded and Samira got to her knees, readying herself to go back into the cave. She was reaching for the first branches when she stopped herself and patted her pants pocket for the lighter.

Cam held it out to her.

She took it without a word, then disappeared into the cave.

He grabbed some more of the branches, brought them into the cave and dropped them by the firepit. No reason for her to crawl all the way back to the entrance for them.

When all the branches were in the cave, Cam went outside to wait. Ripped a piece of timothy grass from between two rocks so he could chew on the stem while he waited.

Time stretched.

Samira didn't return.

How long did it take to dump a bunch of branches?

Cam felt his irritation and unease growing again.

What the hell was she doing back there anyway?

Cam didn't think he wanted to know.

27

But then it came to Cam—she was probably praying for Ambar. Holding a memorial service for one. Kind of like what he had done, just moments before. But probably a lot better.

He eyed the sky. Clouds were moving in. Big, honking dark ones.

Great. Just what they needed now: a mountain squall.

Squalls were common as dirt up here—amazing they hadn't gotten dumped on already.

Still no sign of Samira.

"Samira?" he called out reluctantly. "The weather's changing. A storm's coming through. Are you almost done?"

She surprised him—at his side before he'd even realized she'd emerged from the cave. Silent as a deer.

"Thank you for letting me look after him," she said. "Now I feel like we can leave him."

"That's good," replied Cam. "But now we've got trouble." He pointed to a thunderhead that was approaching fast. "We've got ten minutes, maybe not even, before that thing turns the taps on us. Whatever happens, we can't let ourselves get caught in it—not without having any dry clothes to change into."

Samira shrugged. "I don't mind getting wet. I won't melt."

Cam shook his head. "You're not in India anymore, Samira.

Getting wet in these mountains is deadly. You get chilled, and it takes only a few hours for hypothermia to set in. That might even have been what happened to your friend—"

"Ambar," Samira said.

"Yeah. Ambar. I was thinking. He might have done what you did—tried to get away from the runners. Or maybe he just got separated by accident. Who knows? But once he was lost, he was screwed. No camping stuff. Nothing to make a fire with. He could have stumbled onto the cave, hoping that would keep him safe for the night. But if he'd gotten caught in the rain, or snow even, and the temperature dropped like it does here at night, well, he'd be toast, so to speak."

Her eyes widened in dismay.

"Sorry," he said. "It's just…"

A fat raindrop plopped into the dirt at Cam's feet.

"So you are saying we are stuck here."

He checked the sky again. *Damn!* He could see the sheets of rain approaching. It would be on them any second.

"Yeah. At least 'til the rain stops."

"And when do you think that will be?" Samira asked.

He saw the fast-approaching line of rain, the deep ranks of low, dark clouds lined up behind it all the way to the horizon.

"I don't know. But it doesn't look good. It looks like we're going to get socked in," he said.

A few more raindrops thudded into the dirt.

He took her arm. "Come on. Get inside. Give me the knife, I'm going to try and grab some firewood before the rain starts for real."

110

Limping, he "ran" to the cover of the brush, began grabbing fistfuls of kindling. Struggled to keep from dropping them all, like the monkey and the peas. Remembered, this time, to dig out some resin from the tree trunks for his firestarter.

The wind picked up. The trees were rustling louder and more wildly as the front passed over them. Then Cam heard the harsh clatter of the rain.

He stuffed the last chunk of resin into his pocket and made a run for it—as fast as his stupid swollen ankle would let him. He was almost at the cave entrance when a gust of wind slashed across his back, bringing driving needles of rain with it.

He ducked inside the cave.

"Whew! That was close!" he said.

"Your hair is wet," said Samira.

He shook his head. Cold droplets of water haloed him and spun away.

"Naah, it's nothing. I made it in time."

But he hadn't—not really. The back of his shirt was wet. And cold, too—the rain was icy.

"It'll be OK. We'll get the fire going and I'll be dry in a jiffy," he said, his voice bouncy with false cheer.

Samira's eyes narrowed, but she didn't say anything. Just took the kindling from Cam's arms and started laying the fire.

He joined her at the firepit.

They heard a *whoosh!* and could see a wall of water curtaining the cave entrance.

Their eyes met.

No need to say what they were both thinking.

28

Samira was standing near the cave entrance, watching the rain cascade in front of it—a watery door through which they could not pass.

"This is like the monsoons we have back home," she said, shivering, "but our rains are warm." She stuck her hand into the veil of water, let the rain caress her fingers. "These feel like…" She drew her hand in quickly, shook it off, wiped it on her pants. "…needles."

Cam joined her at the entranceway. He craned his neck to look up at the sky. What he could see was the colour of lead.

Of snow.

Damn and double damn.

"Yeah, our rains are not exactly a nice, hot, double-stall shower. Especially at this time of year."

"I now understand what you meant about having to stay dry," she said. "I am dry, and I'm cold as it is."

Cam turned to her, gave her thin t-shirt and cotton pants a once-over. *She wasn't dressed for a night in the mountains anymore than her buddy Ambar had been.*

He wished he'd had more time, or had thought faster anyway, and gotten more firewood before the rain had begun. He doubted he'd collected enough to last them through the night.

There were *the boughs they'd used to cover the dead boy...*

He shuddered at the idea.

No. Don't even go there, Cam thought.

"Cam?" Samira was saying. "The rain is doing something strange..."

He looked where Samira was pointing.

The drops had thickened. *Turned to sleet.* In between them, he spied a few fat, wet snowflakes.

His stomach sank.

"That's snow..." Cam said. "You see? Those white things?"

Samira's eyes widened. "Really? It looks like...well, like nothing! Not what I'd imagined at all." Her voice was disappointed, like a kid at Christmas unwrapping a toy she did not want.

"That's because it's still more rain than snow," Cam explained. "If it gets colder though, it will change, and you'll see, it will look more like what you imagine. Big, fat, fluffy flakes that stick on everything they touch."

She gave a little skip, almost, and grinned at him. "I can't wait to see that."

Cam was about to tell her not to be so anxious, that if the rain turned to snow, that was bad news for them, but he stopped himself. Remembered how she reacted the last time he pointed out the obvious: *"Are you* trying *to terrify me?"*

No, he decided. Reminding her of how crappy things looked right now wouldn't change anything. It would just make them both feel awful. Besides, why *shouldn't* she get a kick out of seeing snow for the first time? It might also be her last time.

It might be *his* last time too.

113

"Come away from here," Cam said. "It's chilly. We have to stay warm."

She smiled at him again, a large, genuine, full-on smile. She let Cam take her hand and lead her back to the firepit. "Will you help me make my first snowball?" she said.

He smiled back. "Sure," he said. "And your first snowman, too."

She giggled.

"And if you're a very good girl, I'll even teach you how to make a snow angel."

"A snow angel? What's that?" Samira asked.

"Ahh!" He cocked his eyebrow at her. "It's something we all used to like to do when we were kids. Like this. You lie down on the ground—" Cam got down to demonstrate "—and move your arms and legs back and forth like this." He scissored his arms and his legs against the rock floor. He lay on the ground for a moment, hands clasped over his head.

When she smiled at him like that, she really looked amazing...

"And when you get up, ever so carefully,"—he mimed painstakingly lifting himself out of the snow—"you leave behind an angel, with wings and a skirt, in the snow."

Samira laughed. "I'd love to make one!" she said.

"I bet you'd make a gorgeous angel," he said without thinking. Immediately felt like an idiot.

Especially since she had that weird look on her face.

Quick. Change the subject.

"You cold?" he asked.

"A bit," she admitted.

"That's not good. We have a long night ahead of us." He plunked himself down on one of the rock "chairs" at the firepit. "Here—snuggle up next to me," he said, patting the stone beside him. "I'll warm you up."

She shot him a suspicious look.

"Samira. Trust me. I'm not hitting on you, OK? Not right now, anyway. We *have* to stay warm. So scoot on next to me. I promise I'll keep my hands to myself."

She bit her lip. Then she slid her bum closer to Cam's and nestled inside his arm.

Her warmth against his body felt good. Very good.

He'd been shivering, too, he realized. Not a lot, but enough to be wary of.

He thought of the dead boy in the back L. Then pushed the thought away, hard.

29

How long could they go before lighting the fire?

The rain had been coming down unceasingly for hours. Although the light that filtered into the cave had dwindled, it wasn't yet dark—Cam estimated the time to be around five o'clock. Still a long way 'til morning.

He surveyed the small pile of kindling Samira had stacked in the pit. She had laid the lighter alongside it, ready for when the time to light it came.

Whatever time that was, Cam didn't think their fire would burn for much more than an hour.

Samira was curled up beside him, her head in his lap, her eyes closed. He liked the way it felt to have her there, his arm draped protectively across her shoulders, resting on her thigh.

He studied her face. It was peaceful now. It was good to see her like that. When her features relaxed, she was awfully pretty.

They had talked for a long while, after Cam had shown her how to make a snow angel. They talked about their lives, about what it was like to grow up in India for her, and in Canada for him, about stupid movies they'd seen and songs they both knew. They tried to sing a few together, but that was a disaster. It was hard to decide whose singing voice was worse! They'd even played a few games, like that one "I'm going on a picnic and I'm going to bring apples, bananas, cantaloupes…" They even managed to laugh. A lot. Despite everything.

But as the afternoon dragged on, there were longer and longer silences between them: silences that stretched dangerously before one or the other jumped in with a silly story or a pathetic knock-knock joke, to try and keep the other's spirits up.

Eventually, though, their words just ran out. The good ones did, anyway. All they had left between them were dark, frightening ones.

Like: *Would they have enough wood?*

Like: *Were they going to die?*

Better to say nothing.

Cam weighed his options. They were slim pickings. Light the fire now, and fight off the chill before it really set in their bones? Or wait as long as possible before setting the precious twigs ablaze?

If the rain stopped, he'd be able to get more wood when they ran out. But if it didn't stop? Then what?

He listened to the steady drumming of the rain outside the cave. A solid British Columbia rain. Cam knew it could rain like that for hours.

Better not hope for the chance to get more wood. Better wait to light the fire, then—

"Cam?" Samira said, her voice a will-o'the-wisp.

"Yeah?"

"Is it suppertime yet?" She was clutching one of the bags of nuts in her fist, holding it up for Cam to see.

He gave her shoulders a squeeze. "Sure. I think we both could use a little snackie about now."

Her fingers were shaking as she ripped open the bag. Her nails had a bluish tinge to them.

When Cam took the proffered cashews from her hand, her fingertips were like ice.

"Nom nom nom," he said, trying his darnedest to keep things light. "Me like cashew."

She slipped a nut between her teeth, held it there, poised between her lips like a small tongue.

Then snap! She drew it into her mouth like a lizard, and gave it a solid crunch.

"My mother and I used to play a game when I was little. She'd put the nut between her teeth, and I'd have to try and get it away from her before she ate it up. She let me win most of the time. But you could never be sure. And it didn't really matter if you won or lost, because you always wound up with a kiss anyway."

Samira smiled, a faraway smile. She slipped another cashew between her teeth.

It was pure impulse that guided him.

Cam leant over and planted his mouth on hers, put his teeth around the nut and bit down.

Samira's eyes widened in surprise, then she yanked her face back from his sharply.

What a jerk and a half he was! How could *he have done that!* Cam was left stupidly holding the nut between his teeth.

To Cam's amazement, Samira collapsed into giggles.

"Oh! Oh!" Samira cried, laughing with such abandon Cam wasn't sure if he should join in, or curl up in a ball and die of embarrassment.

He sheepishly chewed the nut, swallowed.

She looked up at him and burst into another fit of giggles. "Oh, Cam, you should see the look on your face! It's priceless! Don't get angry. You just surprised me, that's all. Here. I'll show you I'm not laughing at you. Try it again. This time I won't let you win so easily."

She slipped another cashew between her teeth, thrust out her mouth and jaw. From behind her clenched teeth, she said, "Come on. Shee if you can get it thish time."

She waited patiently while Cam tried to figure out what to do. This game was sort of like a kissing game, after all…

Maybe?

He leaned toward her. Not sure…

Snurp!

The nut disappeared.

"Too slow," she said.

She placed another nut between her teeth.

"Come on, Cam. Try harder."

This time he didn't hesitate. He just reached around to the back of her head, pulling her in to him while he kissed her.

It probably wasn't the most beautiful movie kiss ever; after all, there was the stupid nut floating back and forth between their mouths like some kind of kidney-shaped ferry boat. But Cam didn't care. He was kissing her, and she was kissing him back, and for the first time in hours, he wasn't cold.

30

They had finally lit the fire.

At first, the heat and flame felt like a party. It felt so good on their faces, and Cam couldn't help but recall that feel-good sense of adventure from the last time he'd lit a fire here, with Dakota, the night they'd slept here.

But the fire was so small. So ridiculously small.

Its meagre warmth wasn't enough to stop the shaking in their bones.

Cam and Samira lay entwined, as close to the fire as they could get without singeing their clothing. Still, they shivered. The bare ground beneath them was as cold as a curling sheet. And even their arms across each other's backs did nothing to keep the chills from wracking their spines. The fire warmed only what it saw, and it saw little beyond the small ring of stones that contained it.

"Do you think we'll make it?" Samira whispered.

"Of course," said Cam, trying to keep his own fear out of his voice. "It's almost morning. And we've made it this far."

"What if it goes out?"

Cam moved his face from behind the veil of Samira's hair so he could see the flames. They were almost spent. Maybe fifteen minutes left—max.

If it went out, they'd be screwed.

They'd been 'lucky' (ha ha) that the rain hadn't turned to snow. But it was still coming down steadily. Not just a squall, like he'd hoped.

As long as the rain kept up, heading out to get more wood was out of the question—he'd never get dry. Even if his clothes stayed dry—like if he stripped down and ran out starkers—he'd never get himself warmed up again.

He doubted he'd have enough strength to get much firewood anyway. Some of his chills were fever chills. That goddammed gash on his leg.

Samira and he had split up the remaining packages of nuts. There had been a total of seventeen cashews for each of them. Not much of a supper. And Cam hadn't had anything to eat since that protein bars last night…Hardly enough calories to keep up the old woodcutting energy.

But there *was* something he could do.

He didn't want to. The idea made him sick.

But if they were talking survival…

Don't think about it. Just do it, he told himself.

He loosened himself from Samira's grasp and rose to his knees.

"We can't let the fire go out." he said. "Stay here."

Understanding dawned on her. She knew where he was going.

Samira looked away from Cam. Nodded once, a short, sharp nod.

Slowly, Cam made his way to the back of the cave. It was

the last place on Earth he wanted to go, he never wanted to even think about that place.

At the bend, he flicked on the lighter. The crystalline walls shimmered, like multifaceted diamonds. Like snow.

At the center of the cave, where once there was a scene of horror, he now saw a scene of profound beauty.

Pine boughs neatly covered Ambar's body, forming a graceful mound. Four X's of wood marked the four corners of his pine-y tomb, and few tangled wildflowers in a clumsy wreath marked its centre.

Samira's handiwork. A work of art.

With a heavy heart, Cam set about dismantling the touching memorial Samira had created. One by one, he lugged the first branches back to the firepit. Wordlessly, she took them from him and began to cut them into smaller pieces.

When he returned for the last time, the fire was leaping and spitting.

"Here," he said. "Put this on."

An expression of horror momentarily crossed Samira's face. But she stretched out her hand and took Ambar's jacket.

"These too," Cam ordered, holding out the dead boy's jeans.

She took them from his hand. Looked away as she wriggled into them, pulling them up over her khakis.

"And these," Cam said.

Ambar's socks. Samira shook her head. "No. You put those on. You need something warm, too."

His stomach lurched at the thought. No surprise that nothing came up, though. He would never let on to Samira, but he had lost his lunch while he was undressing Ambar. It was the sickest thing he'd ever done in his life.

But Samira was right. He could use warmer socks if he didn't want to lose a toe.

Blanking out his mind as best he could, he unlaced his Vans and kicked them off. He forced himself to pull the socks on up over his own. They were tube socks—good thick ones. But when he tried to slip his shoes back on, they didn't fit. Too small with the thick socks.

No. Don't make me go there, he prayed to an absent god.

But he knew he had to. It was the right thing to do. The smart thing.

Wordlessly, Cam passed his Vans to Samira. Then he reached across to where he'd dumped the dead kid's Adidases. They were a size bigger than his own shoes.

He unlaced them methodically. Put them on his own feet. Re-laced them tight. Tried his damnedest not to look at the toes...

The fire crackled. That smell of Christmas again. It should have filled him with cheer, but instead it just made him feel sick, sick, sick.

He lay down beside Samira, shimmying as close to her as he could. Her arms came around him in an embrace and she held him tight.

She was still shivering, even with the fire blazing. Even wearing Ambar's clothes.

Samira searched Cam's eyes with her own. Could she see the pain he felt, the disgust and the sorrow and, yes, the hope too, all tangled together in his soul like a ball of yarn? Could she see what he was feeling now, for her?

As if in answer to his question, she stroked his face, kissed him, and nestled her cheek into his shoulder.

He hugged her even tighter and prayed.

31

It was cold. He couldn't let himself drop off. While Samira slept in his arms, he needed to stay awake to monitor the fire. If it went out, the cave was cold enough for them to wind up with hypothermia. And if that happened, they could die in their sleep. Like Ambar.

But he was tired. So tired.

He kept himself from drifting off by imagining different scenarios in his head. Revisiting conversations in the past that had gone wrong, and what he wished he'd said.

For some reason, his mind kept going back to the stupid fight he'd had with his dad, when he tore out of the house. It had been just one of a million fights the two of them had had, all of them basically the same. His dad trying to lay down the law. And Cam, bristling with attitude, refusing to go along with the program—any program.

His dad had been right this time, though—Cam *had* been slacking off at home. He had forgotten to close the gate. But that's not what their argument had been about. Not really.

Truth was, Cam was pissed off all the time since his dad had taken the job on the pipeline. He was fed up with his dad dumping all the work on the ranch onto Cam's shoulders while he was gone. So his dad was mad about the horse. But Cam was mad about, well, *everything*.

Cam knew, deep down, that his dad didn't really want to be gone so much. That the gas company paid big, and work was scarce these days in town. And yeah, when Cam wasn't so pissed he saw white, he even knew that what his dad was doing made perfect sense. But that didn't mean Cam had to like it. He was fifteen, for Chrissakes. He didn't want to run a ranch. All he really wanted to do was have a little fun. Maybe even go a little wild and crazy now and then, like Dakota got to. Was that really so much to ask?

Maybe. Maybe not.

But as he lay shivering in the cave, all of his old, bitter feelings faded into nothing.

What did they matter, really? What mattered was trying to keep it together, one day at a time.

One night at a time.

He tightened his arms around Samira, not enough to wake her, but just enough so he could really feel her solid presence next to him. Know she was alive. And he was alive, too.

Not much more a guy could ask for, really.

He buried his face in her hair, inhaling its smoky fragrance. He let his eyes close again and inwardly replayed Samira's story, hearing the dark huskiness of her voice in his mind. He listened to her tell again how her dad went off and left her with her aunt. How she described her father's decision. How she'd said "it had been hard on him" when her mother had died.

Cam just didn't get it. Hadn't having her mom die been

hard on her, too? Why hadn't her "loving" father thought of that? And how could he have paid total strangers to take her halfway around the world—illegally?

OK, Samira was right—Cam had no clue what their lives were like over there in India. But there had to have been another way. Didn't the man know what could happen to kids out there on their own? How come if Cam knew how bad snakeheads could be, Samira's own father didn't seem to know—or care?

Compared to Samira's dad, well, his own dad looked like frigging Santa Claus. Sure, he was on his case all the time. But that's because he did care. Deep down, Cam understood that much.

Cam also knew that both of his parents had to be frantic by now. After all, he'd been gone almost two whole nights. They'd be calling out the troops for sure. Yeah, his dad might tar the shit out of him once Cam was found. But he'd never just leave Cam out there, on his own, without doing his damned best to find him, to keep him safe.

Mostly, though, as the long night wore on, Cam thought about Samira, how good it felt to hold her, how much he wanted to take care of her, make her sad life a little sweeter. He let his mind construct elaborate fantasies about what could still happen, if he had the chance. How much he wanted to be with her.

Eventually, a rebellious little idea wormed its way into Cam's mind.

All along, he'd been thinking that Samira would have to turn herself in to the Canadian authorities when they got down the mountain.

But what if she didn't? What if no one knew about her, except him? Samira *could* stay in Grand Forks as long as her presence was kept a secret.

The idea knocked him flat; it took his breath away. She was illegal—true enough. But there were a gazillion illegals in Canada. Living, working, going to school, getting by under the radar. Hell, every other migrant worker picking fruit in B.C. was an illegal immigrant. So why not Samira? If they stayed mum, she could stay as long as she wanted. All he had to do was find her a place to live...

Cam hugged her as tight as he dared. God, how he wanted her to stay! She wasn't like the girls at school. Shoot, none of those girls ever looked at him anyway. But Samira was different. Special. Smart and funny and *real.*

He'd do *anything* to keep her from leaving Grand Forks. Anything...

He buried his face deeper into her hair, struggling to work out what seemed to be an impossible problem. Could she really stay in Grand Forks? Would she *want* to? Would *she* want *him*?

32

The next thing Cam knew, it was morning. He was alive, Samira was alive, and the sun was shining.

He touched Samira's cheek. She opened her eyes, gave him a butterfly kiss on his forehead with her lashes. Then a real kiss, soft as a butterfly's wing, on his lips.

"So we made it, then," she said.

He kissed her back, hugged her tighter. "Seems so," he said.

Samira wriggled out of Cam's grasp, sat up, stretched and yawned.

"How long have you been awake?" Cam asked her. Unable to take his eyes off her.

"Hard to say. I heard birds chirping somewhere. It was still dark, but I knew dawn had to be close once I heard them. I might have fallen asleep again after that. But gosh. I'm hungry. Cold, too. But hungry more than anything."

Cam poked at the fire. The embers were still glowing.

"So let's go hustle us up some eggs. Pancakes, too. We can fry them up in a jiffy. Fire's still good to go," he teased.

"Don't say that! You are torturing me," she said, but her grin was anything but tortured.

"I promise you a giant brekkie at Del's when we get into town, then."

Samira crawled to the cave entrance and peered out.

"So do you think it's safe to go, then? Do you think they're gone now?"

Cam came up beside her, put his arm around her shoulder and pulled her in tight to his side.

"What do you think? How long would those guys look for you before they got moving?"

"I don't know...Sandip and Jay would have wanted to hurry up. Kav, though, I bet he's really angry. He'll want to find me. No matter what."

Cam considered Samira's words. There was still a pretty serious risk to leaving the cave. But how long could they stay there without putting themselves in even greater danger? He didn't think they could handle another night on the mountain. Maybe if he hadn't gotten that damned infection on his leg. But as it was...

"Let's go, then." Cam decided. "We'll stay quiet. Keep our eyes and ears open. Stay out of sight. They're probably long gone...slinging down shots in a bar in Seattle already."

Samira eyed him doubtfully.

Cam pictured their possible routes down the mountain in his mind. He pointed out over the valley. "Town is that way. The main trail—the one you guys came up on—runs down over there, through that gully. You can't really see it from here.

"Over this way, toward the east, well, that's where the trail I wrecked my bike on is. There are lots of easy-to-follow animal tracks over there, and plenty of other bike trails too. I know them all pretty well. If we go that way, I think we can steer clear of you-know-who and you-know-who."

"That sounds good," said Samira.

"Even better," Cam said, still thinking, "is that my dad's friend lives out that way. His ranch is the last one out of town, practically up against the foothills. We can head straight there. He's a good guy. He'll be able to help us." Cam nodded sharply to himself, satisfied with his plan. "Yeah. That makes sense."

"Well, then," Samira replied. "Sounds like you've got it all figured out. So what are you waiting for?"

Cam thought of the dead boy at the back. Almost said something, then thought better of it.

"Nothing," he said. "Let's roll."

As they picked their way slowly down the trail, Cam was pleased to discover his ankle was sturdy—practically good as new.

Thank God for small favours, eh? he thought.

After they'd been walking for about ten minutes, Cam heard Samira whisper his name.

"Cam?" Samira said in a small voice. "I'm getting more and more worried. I don't think your authorities will let me stay in Canada. I'm sure they'll deport me."

She turned to Cam and put out a hand to him. Her face was drawn, pinched.

He drew her to him and circled her with his arms. Pulled her so close he thought she'd have to feel the sick thudding of his heart, its jagged bass line tantamount to a confession that he'd been worrying about the very same thing.

"*Naaah.* Everything's going to be fine," he told her. He stroked her hair, bent to kiss her face, wanting nothing more than to pretend the anxiety away, to pretend they were just taking a stroll on a spring day, and not just running headlong from one danger into another.

But Samira wasn't very good at denial. She held up two fingers and placed them against his lips. Looked him squarely in the face.

"You don't know that, Cam. Let's face the facts. The most likely thing to happen is they will put me on a plane back to India before the week is out. But I don't want to go back. Not now! I've come so far, been through too much to give up. I want to see my father again. I want to..." Her face crumpled.

"No! Shh! Don't cry. Please don't cry..." Cam said, his voice breaking. "You're right. It's true. Neither one of us knows what's going to happen once we get back to town. But I can promise you one thing: Whatever it is, you won't be alone."

He took her face in his hands and tipped it so their eyes met. "We're in this together. From now on. OK?"

She smiled a sad smile.

"OK?" Cam repeated. "Samira? We're in this together." He kissed her, then kissed her again, kissing away her tears and her worries and his own dark fears. "I promise. Together. You and me."

"OK! OK!" Samira said, laughing through tears, pushing him away. "We're together. You've made your point. I'll try not to fret too much. Not until we get to your town, at least."

"Good. That's a start, anyway," he said.

Cam snapped his fingers. "I got it—why don't you pray to the Lord Whootsie you were talking to yesterday. Tell him to look out for us. Or I'll give him what for." He clowned a little, pretending to box with the sky.

"Shh...You're being bad..." Samira said. "It's never good to make fun of the gods." But she giggled anyway. "And it's Lord Ganesh. Not Lord...whatever you said."

Cam felt the knot in his gut loosen as she smiled up at him.

"All right then. Let's just focus on the here and now." He cleared his throat and mimicked a TV announcer's voice, "It's a beautiful day in the Kootenays, and our hero and his girl are enjoying a leisurely stroll through the glorious countryside before returning to their villa for a sumptuous breakfast of eggs and pancakes..."

"Enough with the eggs and pancakes talk already!" Samira laughed.

"Fine. Then you fill in the blanks." He switched to the smarmy announcer voice again: "Our hero and his girl are returning to their villa for—"

"A dip in their gold-tiled swimming pool," Samira offered.

"Nice," Cam said, grinning.

Samira stopped short. Her face went white. "Did you hear that?" she whispered.

Cam instinctively crouched down and backed off the trail into the brush. He listened hard.

Voices.

33

"Oh my God! It's them!" Samira said, her hand covering her mouth. She looked like a terrified hare, ready to dart.

But it wasn't them. Cam could tell by the rhythm of the voices—they were locals. His shoulders relaxed. "Nah. It's just some guys out for a hike."

Samira listened harder. She slumped against Cam.

"Yeah, *Bhagwan ka shuker hai*. You're right. Those voices don't sound familiar. I thought I was going to faint for a second."

But Cam was still listening. He knew those voices...at least one of them.

"Holy crap. I can't believe it!" he whispered. "Of all the..."

"What?" Samira asked.

"I think one of those guys is an old buddy of mine. Dakota. We used to hang together. He was the guy I camped with. In the cave."

Samira's eyes brightened. "That's great! We could certainly use a helping hand about now!"

Cam didn't move.

"So? What are you waiting for?" Samira asked.

"I dunno...it's kind of complicated," Cam replied.

Samira studied his face, her brow furrowed. "They're heading this way," she said. "Cam?"

Cam was trying to work out what to do.

It was true—they *could* use help getting home. But he didn't want to have to explain about the traffickers and Samira to Dakota. He didn't even want to *introduce* Samira to Dakota. Dakota could be such a…

He could hear the guys approaching. See them through the trees.

Yup, it *was* Dakota. He'd recognize that faded jean jacket anywhere. But the other guys? Not a clue.

Black leather, head to toe. They looked like bikers. One even had a grayish rectangle of a beard sticking out from his chin like a fuzzy ruler.

What was Dakota doing with these guys? Shouldn't he be in his usual place, hanging in front of the school, like every other morning?

Dakota was saying to the guy with the beard, "Look—you see where the trail cuts down around that boulder? That's the border. We're practically there now. So can we turn back now? I got things to do, dude."

The guy with the beard said, "Shut the fuck up, twerp. We'll go when I say we go."

Fear jangled in Cam's gut. Whoever these guys were, they were trouble.

Cam glanced over at Samira—her eyes were wide. He could read their uncertain expression easy as pie: "*You're kidding me! These guys are 'friends' of yours?*"

He gave his head a tiny shake—enough to let her know to stay quiet, that he'd explain later.

Dakota, cocksure as always, said, "Chill, Rocks! Give it a rest."

"No. Why don't *you* give it a rest," said the second biker.

"Hey!" Dakota squeaked. Through the trees, Cam could see the man had grabbed Dakota by his jacket's collar. Was literally holding him off the ground so his toes barely brushed the dirt.

Then there was a sudden flurry of motion. Cam heard fists sinking into flesh, and an *oof!* as Dakota took a hard punch to the gut. Then came the sickening crunch of something solid—a club? a gun butt?—as it made contact with Dakota's face.

"That's enough," said Rocks, his voice unperturbed, as Dakota lay gasping and choking on the ground. "You've made your point, Mal."

"He's been freaking getting on my nerves the whole way up here," insisted Mal. "He needs to be told, man."

"Yeah well, consider your message delivered," replied Rocks. He bent down and grabbed Dakota roughly by the ear. "Listen, dickwad," he said, "don't forget it was your big mouth that got you this 'field trip.' So here's your lesson of the day: keep your fricking mouth *shut* if you don't want stuff like this to happen to you."

He backhanded Dakota hard across the face.

Dakota yelped in pain and surprise. He tried to cover his face with his hands, but Rocks put his beefy forearm across them, holding them down.

"And here's your homework. Keep your trap shut. We don't like to leave bodies lyin' around. Gets too messy. But we will freaking throw your sawed-up corpse over this here cliff if we have to. In actual fact, Malcolm here would get off on doing it. Right, Mal?"

Malcolm cracked his knuckles and grinned.

Rocks backhanded Dakota again. "So when you get back to town, *Dick*ota, you will tell your Borsht Bowl playmates that we weren't such badasses after all. We just hung out, had a beer, smoked some weed. Good times. But if you call the cops like some kind of a-hole, or if you or your pals breathe one word of this to anybody, you will be blood-splatter before the day is out. This is the gospel truth. Right, Mal?"

"Gospel. Hail Mary and amen," said Mal. "God save the queen. *Jah mahn.*"

Rocks shook Dakota hard. "IS THAT CLEAR, dickhead?"

Cam heard Dakota mumble something, and saw Rocks nod.

"Good. Then I'll just give you a little goodbye prezzie to remind you I'm fricking serious."

Rocks got to his feet. Without warning, he swung his leg. His boot connected with a *crack!* into the side of Dakota's head.

Dakota's limp body spun sideways, hit the ground, and then was still.

34

"Funny, this twerp's *still* annoying. Even when he's out cold," said Mal. "Can I? Can I please? Just once?" He held up his boot, wiggling his foot in the air.

"Leave him," Rocks said.

Malcolm sighed. "All right. But gimme just one sec—I gotta clear my throat," replied Mal. He horked up a wad of phlegm from deep in his lungs, and then spit on Dakota's inert body.

"OK. I'm ready now," Mal said.

They left Dakota lying in the dirt. With the chains on their leathers clanking and their voices boisterous and crude, they headed back down the mountain the way they came.

As soon as they were out of sight, Samira started to her feet. Cam caught her eye and held one finger to his lips. They had to sit tight, stay quiet, until the men were out of earshot.

She blinked her acknowledgement and stayed still.

When Cam was certain the bikers were gone, he scrambled out of the brush and ran, limping, down to Dakota.

Dakota still wasn't moving. Out cold.

"Dakota! *Dakota!*" Cam said, shaking him lightly. "Buddy, talk to me. You OK?"

Dakota opened his eyes, started, then groaned. "*Faaaah…!*"

He brought the back of his hand across his mouth. It came away covered with blood and spit.

"Cam. Crap. What the hell are *you* doing here?" he asked through bloody spit bubbles.

"I could say the same to you," Cam replied. "You OK?"

Dakota sat up, shook his head a few times, and blinked.

"Yeah, I'm OK. My head is full of stampeding stegosaurs, but I'll live."

Samira said, "Thank God you're all right. I thought that man was going to kill you!"

Dakota turned to look at Samira, his mouth gaping in surprise. "Who the hell is she?" he asked Cam.

"Her name's Samira," Cam replied. "Can you stand up, D?"

"Hey, hey. Lemme go, Cam! You're like a freakin' mother hen. Yeah, I can stand. It's not like he broke my leg or anything. Just gave me a wee pounding, friendly-like."

Cam made a dismissive noise, a kettle hissing. "More like he used your melon like a soccer ball, dude. I wouldn't be surprised if you have a concussion."

Dakota got to his feet. Brushed himself off. Spit on the ground—a great gob of saliva and blood.

"Sorry," he apologized to Samira. "Not my best gent behaviour." He rubbed his jaw. "Luckily that clam didn't include a tooth."

Samira didn't say anything. Gave Cam that look again: the *so*-this-*is-your-friend?* look.

"I told you it was complicated," Cam said to her.

35

"So, you two lovebirds just taking a romantic walk in the country?" Dakota asked.

"Eff off, Dakota," said Cam. "Who the heck were those guys?"

Dakota clicked his tongue on the roof of his mouth dismissively.

"Just your average ripper-gangbanger-meth-head creeps. Not my first choice of company for a fine Tuesday morning such as this."

Dakota's words sounded flip, but Cam could see that Dakota was faking his bravado. He'd gotten a pretty bad beating back there; he was holding his ribs like they hurt when he breathed. Bruised for sure, maybe even broken.

But Dakota was Dakota—filled to the brim with B.S. No surprises there.

"So! Samira…Is that what my buddy here said your name was? How'd Cam luck into meeting a hottie like you?"

Samira eyed him coolly. Not impressed. She just clamped her lips tighter, took three long strides to put herself ahead of the boys, and kept walking.

Dakota turned to Cam, one eyebrow raised. "Oooh. A cool customer. Nice." He drew out the last word like a hiss: *Niccccccccceeeee.*

"Is she new in town? Don't remember seeing her around the halls of good old G.F.H.S."

"She can tell you about herself if she wants to," Cam said. "But come on, Dakota. You owe us an explanation."

"Says who? Didn't you hear 'em tell me to keep my mouth shut?" Dakota asked.

"Well, it's a little too late for that, isn't it? We've already heard plenty. So just go ahead and spill."

Dakota sighed. "All right. Here's what happened. But you gotta promise to keep this to yourselves."

"You know you can trust me," said Cam.

Dakota's eyes met Cam's then slid away. "Yeah. I know," he said. He pointed to Samira. "But what about her? I don't know her from Adam."

"I heard what those men said," said Samira, slowing down. "I don't want to be 'blood-splatter' either. I promise—I won't say a word."

They walked a few steps in silence.

"So you know I started running bud," Dakota began.

Cam gave the slightest nod of his head in acknowledgement. Yeah, he knew.

"The money was frigging awesome," Dakota continued. "And it was easy as shit. All I had to do was go over to the house past the MacLellan place—you know it, Cam, the ranch with the three Rottweilers? Used to scare the crap out of us. Never ever saw the people there—they'd just leave a couple of hockey bags for me, already packed with weed and ready to go out on the back porch.

"I'd hump them one at a time up the hill and chuck 'em over the border. No sweat—the bags hardly weighed more than our packs did up at that boy scout camp, remember? The smell kinda got to me after a while, though—some serious weed reek. Makes you want to puke, but whatever.

"To dump the bags, I'd use the GPS on my phone. Go to 'predetermined coordinates.' Getting where you had to go was the worst part—sometimes you had to bushwhack through fricking jungly shit. Once I was there, I'd take a look around, make sure there was nobody in sight. *As if.* Then I'd just toss the bag under a tree. Pick up an envelope with a tidy sum o' cash in it when I got back. I did five runs right after school started. Made enough dough to buy an iPod and keep it stocked with new tunes for the rest of my life. I'm thinking of buying a car now."

"None of that explains your two buddies," said Cam.

"Chillax...I'm getting to that," said Dakota, wheezing slightly. "I was sitting with my boys at the Borsht Bowl. Having some breakfast before checkin' into homeroom. Or not." Dakota's face bore a sly expression. "Tatlow, Thiessen, you know, those guys."

Cam nodded. He knew them—skeezbags from school.

"We were eating our eggs and shooting the shit about how easy this bud-running was. How we wished we'd got onto it sooner. What the best routes were, what kind of gear we were using. Like, Tatlow has this funked-out app on his phone that tells him if the plant he just waded through was poison oak. *Sweet.*

"Well anyway, this biker dude was sitting in the booth behind us. Eavesdropping. Don't say it, Cam. I know, you're right. You always used to say to me, 'your mouth's gonna get us into trouble.'"

"Um, *yeah*. Like every day," Cam said, shaking his head, remembering.

"Well damn, if you weren't right." Dakota slapped Cam across the back, harder than was necessary. "Anyway, the dude gets up, leans over the back of my booth, breathing down my neck, and he's like, 'Sounds like you boys can be a big help to me and my pals.'"

"You saw him—he was a serious bad dude. Thiessen looked like he was pissing his pants, he was so scared. I would have laughed, but that's when tat boy puts his hand on my shoulder. He goes, 'Since you're such an *expert*, why don't you show me your route through the mountains?'

"You saw him, Cam. He's the size of a goddamn kaibo. So I just nod and get to my feet. I reach into my pocket to grab a couple of loonies, but the guy grabs my wrist. He goes, 'Your crew is only too happy to buy us all breakfast. Right, boys?' Tatlow and Thiessen just nod like freakin' bobbleheads.

"So he takes me out to his truck. There's this meth-head dude waiting in there—Malcolm, my guy calls him. He makes me get in the back and tells me not to piss off Mal 'cause he has a bad temper. Mal was gross, man. He had, like, total meth-mouth. Ugh. I wanted to crack a joke but thought I'd better not."

"Never too late to learn," Cam said dryly.

"Yeah, you are *so* right. Live and learn. That's my new motto, baby. Live and learn. So I'm sitting there in the back seat, freaking, like, where're they gonna take me? So I'm trying to keep my cool, make some convo, you know, keep it light, find out what I can. Ask Tat-boy his name. He tells me I can call him Joe Rocker, *ha ha*, like the brand of the damn motorcycle boots he's wearing, and if I don't shut up I'll be wearing them on my face."

"He the one with the beard?" Cam asked.

"Yeah. So I zip it. Jesus, I thought for sure they were gonna kill me and leave me for dead in a gully somewhere. But it turns out they just want me to show 'em a couple of trails up through the mountains. Their gang is planning on moving in. They're going to rip whatever they can this summer. And they wanted to 'reconnoiter'—yeah, he actually said 'reconnoiter', as I live and breathe. Who'da guessed he could string together four whole fricking syllables? And there I was, right time, wrong place, shooting off my mouth about how many paths I knew through the hills, yadda yadda."

"You're lucky they didn't kill you," Samira said.

Dakota's eyes dropped. "Yeah. I know."

Cam said, "I told you should stay away from that kinda sh—"

Dakota held up his hand. "Spare me the lecture, Cam. OK? I got it." He rubbed his jaw, where a large purple bruise was forming. "I promise I'll be a good boy from now on. Scout's honour." He put three fingers up in the scout salute. Then, laughing, he bent down his two outside fingers, leaving just the middle finger up.

144

36

"You're an idiot," Cam said.

"News flash," Dakota replied. "But hey, I'm *your* idiot. At least until we get down the mountain. So, Samira, feel like catching a flick when we get back into town? Maybe get a burger or sumptin'?"

Samira looked at Cam. "Can you do something to stop him from talking?"

Cam laughed. "Believe me, I've tried. Never worked."

She sighed. "Dakota, please shut up. You give me a headache," she said.

"Well la-di-*dah*!" Dakota replied, putting on a mincing walk.

Samira stopped in her tracks. Her eyebrows drew together in a scowl. "Look, I don't care who you are or what your story is. But here is *my* story. We are hungry. We are tired. We need to get off this mountain right away. I don't have any patience for your 'smart guy' attitude. Is that understood?"

Dakota just cocked his eyebrow.

"Well? Is it?" she demanded.

Dakota turned to Cam, pointing at Samira with his thumb. "Where did you find this one?"

Cam just stared at Dakota. Then he replied, "Like she said,

145

Dakota. We're not in the mood for your crap. So if you're going to hike down the mountain with us, turn off your mouth. Or go find your own trail."

A small, wry smile began to curl Dakota's lip. "Whoa...she's got you whipped, buddy."

Cam turned on his heel and said, "Come on, Samira, let's go."

They were about twenty yards down the trail when they heard Dakota call out, "Hey! OK. Sorry. I'm sorry, OK? I'm a freaking idiot, you are right. And maybe I'm even a bigger tool than usual cuz I can barely think straight. My head is throbbing like a bass drum. I promise though, I'll be a good boy 'til we get back to town. Just don't leave me, all right? I can barely fricking breathe."

Cam looked back over his shoulder at Dakota. He was white. Wincing, clutching his ribs.

Cam touched Samira's arm. She slowed her pace, looked back at Dakota, too. Saw what Cam saw—a kid who had just had the crap kicked out of him. A kid who looked like he was going to fall down any second.

Without them, there'd be no one to catch him when he did.

Samira muttered something to herself in Hindi. Then out loud she said, "Fine. But don't expect me to like you. And no talking."

Dakota breathed a sigh of relief. He ambled up alongside Cam. "Good. Glad that's settled." He tried to smile, but what crossed his face was more of a grimace than a grin.

"So tell me. Why do you have to always be such a pain in the ass?" Cam asked him.

Dakota punched him in the arm. Weakly.

"Admit it. It's what you love about me. Dude! Admit it! Pain-in-the-ass-ness is what I'm all about."

Cam just sighed and kept walking.

37

"**W**hat I don't get is why you couldn't just ask your folks for an allowance, D. It's not like they aren't rolling in it," Cam said. Dakota's dad was some hotshot with the gas company. They lived in one of the biggest houses in town, up on 'Snob Hill.' White columns, an Escalade in the driveway.

"Aw c'mon, man. You know my dad. He makes yours look like a pussy*gato*." Dakota puffed himself up and deepened his voice. "'Nobody ever handed me anything on a silver platter, son. Hard work is what you need to make you a man!' You know the drill, Cam."

"Yeah, I know. But even so…Look, Dakota, this drug-running gig—that's serious stuff. You had to know nobody pays out money like that for nothing."

"Give it a rest, Cam. This whole town is swimmin' in bud money. It's simple economics. Supply and demand. Folks demand their smokes, and we got the best damn supply of weed right here in our own backyard. You'd have to be a bonehead to not see the opportunity. So I sized up the situation. And I'm like, 'I'm gonna do exactly what dear old dad suggested. Work hard at something with a future. Face it, dude, the future in B.C. is B.C. bud. We even got a mayor growing the stuff. If you can't smell what's blowing in the wind, Cam, you need some Benadryl."

Cam felt his jaw tightening. "Not everybody is growing weed," he said. "Or selling it. There are still plenty of people who don't need to mess with that to make a living. An *honest* living."

"Like who? Principal Butthole? I bet even he's got a tidy little hectare or two behind his house—his own personal 'retirement plan.'"

"So what if he does? What *you're* doing is still illegal. And that makes it a bad idea, even if everything else you say is right, which it isn't," said Cam.

Dakota hooted. "You know who you sound like? You sound just like your old man! Self-righteous and tight-assed. Can you hear yourself squeaking, Cammo?"

Cam felt his annoyance at Dakota turn to anger. "Yeah, well, I'd rather be like my old man than like your pal Malcolm the meth-head, or, or—like *you*, Dakota. At least *my* dad believes in something other than making a buck."

"Oh yeah? Since when? You're dad's a freaking tool, man! You've told me so only like a billion times!"

Cam kept his eyes straight ahead, but the tendons in his neck stretched taut, like wire.

"Got nothin' to say? Fine. Whatever," said Dakota. He shook his head and strode on ahead, chuckling softly to himself.

Samira came up beside Cam, slipped her hand into his.

"Don't let him get to you. He's wrong, you know," she whispered in his ear. She gave his hand a squeeze.

They walked on for a while in silence.

Then Dakota slowed up, letting Cam and Samira catch up to him.

"So what's your deal, Samira?" Dakota said, falling into step with them. "I told you my tale of woe. Your turn. 'Fess."

Samira laughed a cynical laugh. "Forget it. You've proven twice today you don't know how to keep your mouth shut. I'd have to be as big an idiot as you to tell you anything. Which I'm not, thank you very much."

"Touché," said Dakota, tipping an imaginary hat at her.

The sun was high above the horizon. They'd been walking for about ninety minutes now and were almost down the mountain.

The realization made Cam's stomach tighten. A new party-pack of worries crowded in on him.

What was he going to do about Samira? Should he keep quiet, try to help her stay in Canada under the radar? Or should he bring her straight to the RCMP? She'd be safer, that's for sure, if they played it straight. But the chances that he'd lose her—well, they were too high to even think about.

And what about Dakota? How could Cam explain to anyone about Samira without spilling the beans about Dakota, Joe Rocker, and Malcolm? And if that story came out, wouldn't Samira and he—and Dakota, too—be in even worse danger than they were already? Maybe it would be safer for all of them if Samira just laid low for a while.

Cam wrestled with the possibilities. None of them looked good.

As they walked, the footpath gradually grew wider and more level. The evergreens thinned as they approached the valley floor, where meadowlands clung to the base of the foothills. Before long, their dusty trail joined up with a larger one that angled from the southeast—the main trail that led back toward Grand Forks.

They'd be at the Crowsnest Highway in less than an hour. For Cam, that wasn't nearly enough time. Not to solve the problem of what to do.

He was still lost in thought when Samira grabbed his hand. "Cam," she said urgently. "Look."

She was pointing to the sky over the mountain. There were helicopters circling.

Cam realized he'd been hearing the *thrum* of their blades for some time without really noticing them.

"What are those for?" she asked. Her voice was tight, anxious. *Scared.*

Cam shrugged his shoulders. "I don't know. Search and Rescue, maybe. Maybe they're even looking for me. I've been gone for two days."

Dakota squinted up at the sky, shielding his eyes with one hand.

"That ain't no search and rescue team, Cammo." Dakota said. "Those birds are Border Patrol. *U.S.* border patrol." A weird look crossed his face. "I wonder what they're doing over here..."

Samira gasped. "Border Patrol? Oh no! They're looking for me!"

Without warning, she bolted. Running as if her life depended on it, she headed back the way they had come, then off the trail and into the cover of the brush.

38

"What the...?" said Dakota, mouth agape.

"Long story," shouted Cam, as he took off after Samira. "Samira! Stop! You're going the wrong way! We're almost at the ranch I told you about. We can go there. Samira! Come back!"

Samira stopped. Her body was rigid, her fists clenched at her sides. Her eyes were so round that Cam could practically see the whites all the way round her irises—that deer-in-the-headlights look. He could hear her breathing, small, rapid gasps that made her chest rise and fall erratically.

Cam realized she was caught up in blind, paralyzing panic—too exhausted and overwhelmed to think straight anymore.

"Don't worry," he said encouragingly. "I'll take care of you! But come on, stay with me. Running off that way won't solve anything."

Dakota was shaking his head. "Why would U.S. Border Patrol be looking for her? Over here? That makes no freaking sense," he said.

"She was part of a group being smuggled into the U.S. by traffickers," Cam said shortly. "They're probably looking for all of them." He jogged over to Samira. "Come on. Let's go," he said gently. "We're almost there. We'll get you warm and dry in a jiffy."

Dakota trotted along behind Cam. "Even so. Those guys

shouldn't be over *here*. Not on *our* side of the mountain. That's not how things are done. Trust me, I got the full low-down on how border enforcement teams work when I started this gig. The U.S. guys don't come over here, and our guys don't go over there."

"Yeah, well. We all know things don't always work how they're supposed to all the time," said Cam. He turned to Samira. "Here—take my hand. All we have to do is get across this little stream. The water's not real deep now. We can wade across."

She took his hand and walked with him like a zombie. Totally spent.

Those damned copters, Cam raged inside, *giving her a scare like that, after she'd had just about as much as she could take, and then some. And if Dakota was right, and they didn't even* belong *here...*

He looked up to check where they were. The helicopters were heading east along the front of the mountain range. Toward them.

Cam wondered if the officers inside them really were searching for Samira. If so, then he had even less time to come up with a plan to keep her safe than he'd thought.

He'd figure out a way to make it work, for both of them. He *had* to.

The thrum of the choppers grew louder.

First things first. Cam chided himself. He had to get Samira out of sight, before they were caught, or there'd be nothing to figure out. The two of them could talk about things then.

Cam gripped her fingers in his and waded into the Kettle River. She followed him without complaint, even though the water was high and flowing fast. It was icy cold, too, and littered with rocks that made the going treacherous. It was tough to keep his footing, to make sure his weak ankle didn't give out on him. But even as he focused on the task at hand, he couldn't stop his mind from whirring:

Maybe Dakota could help us...He probably knew people who'd be happy to give Samira a bed, no questions asked, as long as she paid her way. Paid her way...Christ! How would she do that? She'd be freaking illegal. Not exactly a candidate for the A&W drive-thru...

Answer: Cam would have to get her the money she'd need. He'd do the A&W gig if he could get it.

As if.

He has already up to his eyeballs with chores at home. And his dad was seriously on his case about his grades. Even if he got some crap job flipping burgers, he could never log the hours he'd need to cover Samira's living expenses. His dad would never let him.

Despair washed over Cam. There was no solution, no logical series of steps that led to X= Samira.

Or was there...?

The pure, perfect equation suddenly fell into place in his mind.

He could do what Dakota had done. Carry a few hockey bags of weed over the border, stuff his pockets with cash...

No: that was just stupid. He'd wind up with the same kind of problems Dakota had.

"Cam!" Samira called out. Her fingers had slipped from his! She was falling, floundering in the freezing water!

"Cam! *Cam!*" she screamed, reaching out for him.

"Hang on, Samira, I'm right here!" he shouted, but his words were drowned by the rush of the water. She was tumbling away, out of his grasp.

39

He stretched his whole body toward her, trying to recapture her hand in his. But then Cam lost his own footing. He was down!

The water closed over his head. It turned him instantly to ice. So bloody cold, Cam felt his lungs seize up and the breath die in his chest.

He floundered, his arms and legs kicking furiously, but he found no purchase. And then his arms just stopped. Paralyzed with cold.

Cam felt himself going down....down...

Omigod, Cam thought, *I'm actually drowning...*

But then he felt a sharp yank on his hair.

Dakota was pulling on it, shouting at him, "Get the hell up, you turd! You're not gonna drown on me, buddy boy, no sirree!"

Cam's head broke the surface. He took a deep aching breath as Dakota clapped him on the back. Then Dakota pushed and pummelled and prodded Cam across the river and up the opposite bank.

But where was Samira? Cam frantically turned his head this way and that, searching for her. At last he spotted her, hauling herself hand over hand along a willow branch that was drooping into the river.

Tougher than she looks, Cam reminded himself. He ran to

her and helped her climb up the bank. Her eyes, when they met his, were black pools of misery.

Dakota, meanwhile, kept glancing anxiously at the sky.

"Those helicopters are a lot closer. Heading this way," he said. "I'm not likin' it. Whoever those guys are, they aren't guys we wanna have anything to do with. I say let's scramble. *Pronto, Tonto.*"

Cam nodded in agreement. "You see that house just over there? That's Tommy Cormorant's place, my dad's friend. C'mon. I'll race you!"

Cam took off like a shot. Samira, too, got to her feet and began to run in the direction of the farmhouse.

40

The farm house was a two-bedroom bungalow trimmed with a green-and-white awning. There were two trucks out front—a 4X4 that Cam recognized as the one belonging to Tommy Cormorant, and an SUV. The garage at the side of the house was open, and Cam could see a pair of ATVs parked inside it.

Cam's burning muscles felt like he'd been running forever, and the house was just as far away as when he'd started. The *thrum* of the helicopters only added to the nightmare feeling. There they were, the three choppers coming up behind him, so close now he could almost make out the facial features of the nearest pilot.

The last helicopter in the line swung around to the right. It sped up. Cam couldn't believe his eyes—there was a man leaning out of the cockpit. And the man was pointing something at him!

Puffs of dirt rose up in a dotted line front of him. A second later he heard it—*thut-a-thut-a-thut-a-thut*—the sound of gunfire!

The guy hanging off of the chopper was shooting at him!

"What the—!" he shouted into the wind. Then he turned on his rockets. Fueled by fear, Cam ran like he had never run in his life. He aimed himself toward the front door of the Cormorant house like a hornet heading for the nest.

His feet thudded up onto the front porch. He practically yanked the screen door off its hinges.

"Samira!" he called over his shoulder.

"I'm right here!" she shouted, a few steps behind him.

He pressed the front door thumb latch and pushed the door open. Thank God it wasn't locked! Together, they stumbled into the house.

But where the hell was Dakota? The way Dakota could usually run, like an antelope, he should have been here first, not pulling up the rear.

Cam peered through the porch window. He scanned the grounds, but saw no sign of Dakota. Just the 'copters swooping toward the farmhouse.

Thut-a-thut-a-thut-a-thut. Puffs of dirt hemmed the front walk.

"Mr. Cormorant!" he called out, looking around the front room. "It's me, Cam Stewart! We need help!"

"What's going on? Where's Dakota?" said Samira at his elbow.

"I dunno! He disappeared. Maybe the helicopters—Samira, they were shooting at us!"

The noise of the copters diminished. Were they flying away?

Cam closed his eyes for a second, trying to get a grip. Then he cautiously edged toward the window. Yeah, he could see the helicopters' tails now—they were leaving.

"Ho-lee crap," he breathed. He slumped to the floor, rested his back against the wall beneath the window.

Dakota was right: Something bizarre was going on. Something way too bizarre for him. Even if the Border Patrol *was* looking for Samira, they shouldn't be shooting at her. *At him.*

Somehow, Cam realized, he had stumbled into something way bigger than they'd bargained for. Cam didn't know what it was, but this much was clear: it wasn't something he could handle on his own. Not when people were shooting at them. Not when Dakota had gone missing. *What if he was lying somewhere, bleeding in a ditch?*

Cam's dream of keeping Samira a secret from the authorities fizzled out.

They had to get help. Now.

No one seemed to be home at the Cormorant place. He looked around the living room for a phone. Saw one sitting on a crocheted doily on a pretty little wooden table.

"I'm gonna call for some help," he told Samira. "You just sit tight. Stay away from the windows."

Cam lifted the receiver to his ear. With a shaking hand, he pressed the digits 9-1-1.

He was listening hard, trying to hurry the connection along with his mind, anxious for the voice of the operator to come on the line and say, 'Grand Forks Emergency Services. State the nature of your emergency and your address, please,' when he heard the screen door slam.

Cam looked up to see who had come in. It was Tom Cormorant!

He breathed a sigh of relief. Help was here!

But then, before the call could go through, Cormorant put one thick finger down across the phone's disconnect button.

"No need for that, son," he said.

41

"Mr. Cormorant! What are you doing? We gotta call 911! We need help! Helicopters are shooting at us! And my friend, Dakota—"

"Not another word, Cameron! Now just do what I say. You too, little lady. And don't try anything funny. I'm *not* happy to see you, and that *is* a gun in my pocket."

A cold sweat broke out all over Cam's body. "I don't understand..." he said, blinking.

Cormorant drew the gun and pointed it at Cam and Samira.

"Do you understand *now*, Cameron?" Cormorant exhaled slowly. "Look. I don't want to do anything we'll both regret, y'hear? So just keep quiet, son. Both of you—on your feet. Hands in the air. Turn around."

Cam stared at his father's friend in disbelief, too numb with shock to move. *Had the whole world gone crazy?*

"Hurry it up, Cameron," Cormorant said, and Cam saw the tip of the gun jerk.

Cam raised his hands over his head and turned around.

Behind him, he could hear Cormorant moving around, doing...something. Just as Cam thought about trying to take a quick look over his shoulder to see what Cormorant was up to, he felt the warm barrel of the gun press into the nape of his neck.

161

"Now Cam, you're going to do what I tell you, nice and easy. You're going to take this rope"—Cormorant dangled a length of blue nylon rope, about as long as his arm, in front of Cam—"and tie up your little girlfriend. And you're not going to let those whirly-wheels in your head tell you to try and do something brave and dumb, like throw the rope at me or try and run for it. This gun has a hair trigger—and I've got one myself, right about now."

Reluctantly, Cam did he was told. As gently as he could with his fumbling fingers, he tied Samira's wrists together in front of her.

"Make those knots good and tight now, son," Cormorant said.

Cam tightened up the knots, silently sending Samira his apology with his eyes.

Cormorant said to Cam, "Get down on your stomach. Hands behind your head."

As soon as Cam was down, Cormorant sat on his back, and whipped a second length of rope around Cam's wrists. He cinched the rope tight, Then Cormorant swivelled and did the same to Cam's ankles, binding them together with another length of rope.

As soon as Cormorant was off his back, Cam rolled over to face him. "So why are you doing this?" he blurted out.

"It's all because of Dakota we're in this mess." Cormorant spit the words out like they were poison. "I should have known better than to hire a Snob Hill kid. Now, Missy, I'm pointing the gun right at your boyfriend. You can turn around and see for yourself."

She turned slowly and let out a gasp when she saw Cam tied up on the floor, with Cormorant pointing the gun at his right eye. She whispered, "What do you want me to do? Only, don't hurt him."

"That's a good girl. A smart one, too. Come sit yourself down on the chesterfield." Cormorant told her.

Samira did as she was told.

Meanwhile, Cam's mind was whirring frantically, trying to make sense of their situation.

"Dakota works for you?" Cam asked as Cormorant began tying Samira's feet. "You don't mean—you're the one he's—you've been growing B.C. bud?"

Cormorant said, "Yeah, I do mean. It was supposed to just be a bit of cash on the side, nice and easy. Needed a strong pair of legs to haul my crop out for me. So I put the word out, and the kid shows up one day. Cockiest little son of a bitch I ever met. Says he can do it. Yeah, well, he did it all right."

Some puzzle pieces fell into place in Cam's mind. "You own that place out near the McLellans?" he asked Cormorant.

"Yup. I got property all over this town. I'm a regular real estate speculator," he said to himself, shaking his head. "Never would have imagined it, in the old days."

"You must be making a mint," Cam said.

Cormorant gave Cam a hard stare. "Yeah, well, nothing's as easy as all that, is it? But things were going along OK until Dakota showed up. Next thing I hear is Dakota's telling half the goddamn town about how sweet he's got it. And he's walking around, waving his fancy little gadgets around saying 'Nope, my daddy didn't buy me nothing. I won the lotto *nudge nudge wink wink*.' Might as well have stood up on the fire tower with a bullhorn and shouted 'I'M RUNNING DRUGS.'"

"Dakota says this town is swimming in drug money," Cam said. "So what's the big deal? It's not like he was shouting, 'I'm running drugs for Tommy Cormorant.'"

"Well, he may as well have been. In business, you don't want people looking too close at what you're doing. And I'm not just talking about the law, son. I'm talking about other growers. Middlemen, too. It was only a matter of time before Dakota caught the eye of someone lookin' for easy pickings. Why, all they'd have to do is shake that skinny little punk to find out where my fields were. Then they could parachute in and 'rip' them— harvest my crop before I did and take it for themselves. A whole year of work, *my* work, gone. And I'd have some very, very, *very* unhappy partners. Folks who aren't as laid back as I am.

"And then this morning, lo and behold, one of the guys just happened to see Dakota coming out of the Borscht Bowl and he's with some gangbanger neither one of us had ever seen before. So he gave me a call. Figured Dakota might be taking his new friends on a bit of a sightseeing tour up here, so we've been waiting to see who'd turn up."

"That's all very interesting, but none of that explains why you've got *us* tied up," said Cam.

Cormorant rubbed his broad palm across his face.

"I'm not real happy about this either, son. Practically stroked out when I saw you kids running across my field. Seems you landed in the wrong place, wrong time. To tell you the truth, kid, I hope the worst *isn't* gonna happen here. And I'm going to do my damnedest to not let that happen. But I can't promise. You see, I'm the low man on this operation's totem pole. I just grow the stuff. My partners are in charge of 'security.' They're gonna be the ones who decide what to do with you. A lot will depend on whether they believe you can keep your mouths shut."

He settled himself heavily in the rocking chair next to Cam. He gave both Cam and Samira frank, appraising looks. "Seems to me my partners will think you know way too much to risk it. We'll have to convince them otherwise. But honestly, son? I'm not sure any of us will see the other side of this fine day."

He rubbed his face again. "We don't have long to wait. When I saw those Yank choppers, I didn't know what the hell was happening. Armageddon, it seemed like. So I called the guys. They're on their way now."

"Are you nuts? Untie us, now! There's no reason to just sit here and let them—"

Cormorant placed one heavy hand on Cam's shoulder. "No, son. It doesn't work like that. Not around here. You'll see why— soon enough."

A chilly finger of fear tapped the base of Cam's spine.

42

Cam heard the roar of motorcycles coming up the gravel drive. His stomach turned inside out. He stole a look at Samira; she was sitting perfectly immobile, eyes fixed on her hands. *She had given up.* Seeing her like that made him even more scared.

"Yo!" someone called into the house. Cam could see two men on the front porch, lifting off their motorcycle helmets and wiping their muddy feet on the doormat. *Nice, well-mannered drug runners.*

When they came into the living room, Cam's eyes almost fell out of his head. They both had patches on their sleeves that read CBSA: Canada Border Service Agency.

He couldn't believe it—Cormorant's partners in his drug business were the very guys who were supposed to be *preventing* drug smuggling! One was a guy called French—he coached the high-school soccer team. The other was known throughout town as "Officer Hunko" because all the ladies thought he was majorly handsome.

So much for trusting authority, Cam thought.

The two officers didn't even glance at Cam or Samira as they passed by. 'Officer Hunko' just beckoned with a leather-clad finger to Cormorant as he pulled a chair out from the table.

Cormorant jumped to his feet. He hurried to join them.

"So the top priority," Hunko was saying, "is our two new arrivals. I ran them through the system—the little guy is Malcolm Yellowdog, your basic filth. Out of Penticton. As an officer of the law, I can tell you I don't want scum like him on my patch."

The men laughed, but then Cormorant said, "Whoa! Back up a sec. I'm missing something here. Who in the hell were those guys in the choppers, and what were they doing shooting up my ranch?"

"I'll get to that," Hunko said. "Now the guy with the beard you told me about—incredible but true—he isn't in the system. Doesn't matter who he is, though. He's a gang member, a criminal element. Not the kind of citizen we want in our fine town, is he, boys?"

"Hear, hear," said French.

"So we decided to act fast, hit hard, and not let these gangbangers move in and make our 'jobs' tougher," Hunko said with a wink at his partner.

French took this as his cue to step in. "Right. So we called in some of the other guys on our cross-border team—that's who was in the choppers. The Americans and us, we all work together to keep the border from turning into a sieve. Except where we want it to, eh? So, we gave some of the U.S. guys the 'facts,' on a strictly 'need to know' basis. As in, they don't *need* to *know* about our private business, eh?"

"We told 'em that we spotted three wanted men, armed and considered dangerous, up on the mountain," Officer Hunko added. "And we told 'em that we were overstretched here, and as a result we were giving them authorization to 'do what it takes' to bring those suckers down. Also that no one would say *boo* if our quarry didn't make it back to Grand Forks alive. Even if their copters, *oops*, crossed the border into Canada if they had to."

"What about Dakota?" asked Cormorant. "You don't want him getting shot up there too, now, do you?"

Cam looked up sharply at Cormorant. *So he hadn't seen Dakota, didn't know Dakota was already down the mountain! And neither, then, did Hunko or French…*

Hunko slapped the table. "The key thing to remember is we don't want *anybody* looking too closely at us, now, do we?" He fixed a hard glare on Cormorant.

Cormorant seemed to squirm in his chair as he answered. "Well, no."

"I thought you'd agree. Turns out, though," Hunko continued, "we got ourselves jammed up. Our guys in the sky spotted some action on the ground. Figured it was our gangbangers. So they let some bullets rip. But no. It turns out it's a couple of kiddies playing hide-and-seek in the woods. Which means we now have a Class A Federal Problem on our hands."

Officer Hunko twisted in his chair so he could fix his bright blue eyes on Cam and Samira. He smiled a cold, reptilian smile. "That problem would be the two of you," he said.

Cam's guts turned to water.

"So anyways, we set the Americans straight and sent Roger and Teddy back onto the mountain to finish the job. They're searching the trails up there now. *With enthusiasm, eh?* They told us they'll shoot whoever they find between Grand Forks and the great state of Texas. And you can bet they won't screw up a second time. Not those cowboys."

Samira's body jerked when she heard Hunko's words.

"No! They can't do that!" she cried out. "There may still be other people up there on the mountain! Innocent people! Helpless people!"

"What in the hell are you talking about, girlie?" said Hunko.

Samira told him about the group being smuggled across the border. Her group.

"You can't let them get shot! They don't deserve to die because of, because of..." Samira struggled to find words to describe what was happening.

"Because you guys are crooks," said Cam, unable to hold his tongue any longer.

Officer Hunko fixed his eyes on Cam. "Great. Another kid with a big mouth," he said.

Yeah, well, too fricking bad, Cam thought, glaring right back at him.

French got up from the table, came around behind the sofa and rested his hands on Samira's shoulders. "It must be hard for you to know your friends might fall afoul of the law." He made a clucking sound. "But wait! They should have thought about that *before* they left home and tried to make a mockery of immigration regulations."

Cam saw the tears start to fall from Samira's eyes.

43

"**I** do appreciate your telling us this," said Hunko. "Now we know we don't have to worry about anybody missing *you*. Seeing as you are an undocumented alien. That's one load off. But this other one here—what's your name, boy?"

Cam didn't answer. Wouldn't answer.

Cormorant spoke for him. "This here's Mike Stewart's son. Cameron."

"*Aw shee-it*," French swore. "I know Stewart. He's a stand-up guy."

"That doesn't matter. What matters is how we're gonna keep our business operations out of jeopardy," said Hunko.

Cam shot him a look as full of disgust as he could muster.

"We can make it look like these two got up to something. An accident. Or a suicide pact. Kids these days do all kinds of stupid shit that gets them dead."

French nodded. "Makes sense to me. I say let's wait 'til dark, though." He checked his watch. "Only an hour or so 'til the sun sets anyways."

"How can you let them do this?" Cam shouted at Cormorant. "You've been friends with my dad since you were in high school together—you told me that yourself! And you've known me since I was a baby!"

Cormorant didn't reply. He just swung his hand through the air like he was swatting away a pesky fly. He pushed his chair out from the table and got to his feet.

"Are you boys all right with finishing this thing up on your own?" he asked French and Hunko. "I gotta feed the horses. And check on things up at the north op before it gets dark."

"Yeah. Fine. You skedaddle, Tommy. You done enough today. We'll let you know when this is all over and done with," said Hunko.

Cormorant nodded. "Good."

He disappeared into the kitchen. Then Cam heard the side door slam, and, a few moments later, the engine of the SUV out by the garage spring to life.

French went into the kitchen, where he was making a hell of a noise. Hunko, meanwhile, had kneeled on the floor in front of Cam. He flicked a finger at the rope around Cam's wrists and sighed.

"Amateurs," he sighed. He reached into the pocket of his jacket and pulled out a handful of white plastic strips—nylon handcuffs. He fastened one loop around Cam's ankles and pulled it tight. Then he reached over and did the same to Samira's.

"Yo, French! Get me a knife, will ya?" he shouted.

"Right-o," called French. He emerged from the kitchen with a blade in his hand. He tossed it to Hunko, then planted himself behind the sofa with his beefy arms crossed across his chest.

"Thanks. Hold up your hands," Hunko said to Cam. When Cam didn't comply, Hunko put the knife to Cam's throat. Cam felt it digging into his skin and instinctively jerked away. In that moment, Hunko grasped his hands, cut the bonds, and pulled him up to a sitting position. Then, in one quick, judo-like move, he wrenched Cam's arms so sharply behind his back, he saw stars.

Hunko fastened Cam's hands together and yanked the loop tight. Extra tight, it seemed.

"Always cuff to the rear. Police Academy 101," Hunko said to no one in particular. Then he moved on to Samira. When he twisted Samira's arms behind her, she cried out in pain.

When he had finished, Hunko rose to his feet, his leather pants creaking.

"We're good to go," said Hunko.

French came over and picked Samira up in his sturdy arms. He carried her into the kitchen and returned a moment later without her.

Cam could hear her, though, crying in the kitchen.

He hadn't killed her—yet.

Cam jerked his body as hard as he could and tried to kick French with his joined-together feet.

Hunko laughed at him. "Give it up, boy-o. French has handled tougher meat than you."

But Cam wasn't going to let himself be slaughtered without any fight at all. He bucked and wriggled, trying to prevent French from getting a grasp on his body. But French was stronger, way stronger, than Cam.

French effortlessly scooped Cam up off the floor, tossed him over his shoulder and hauled him into the kitchen. It had been cleared of furniture. Turned into a 'holding cell.'

With surprising gentleness, French put Cam back down on the bare floor.

"Frenchie!" Hunko called from the living room.

"On my way," French called out. Then, without another glance at Samira or Cam, he turned on his heel and strode out of the room.

44

It was twilight. Samira and Cam were lying face-to-face on the cold linoleum. As their eyes met, Cam could see Samira's were full of tears.

"I'm so sorry I got you into this mess," she whispered, her voice breaking.

"You got me into this? Nuh-uh—I think it was me and Dakota that got you all tangled up. You would have been home free if you hadn't met me," Cam replied, his own words sounding hoarse, strangled.

"I guess it really doesn't matter. We're both going to die now anyhow," she said. She choked back a sob, tried to rub the tears off her face using her shoulder.

"Here, lemme," said Cam. He wriggled his body toward Samira until they were touching. He shifted his shoulder and awkwardly wiped her wet cheek on his shirt.

Samira responded by kissing him on the neck, on the face, on the lips.

"I don't want to die!" she said between kisses. She was sobbing openly now, tears pouring down her face as she kissed him.

The lump in his throat was choking him. If only he could hug Samira, wrap his arms around her body and somehow, together, be miraculously spirited away.

"Me neither," said Cam, tears welling in his own eyes. He closed them, squeezing them tight, and fervently kissed her back. To his own amazement, Cam found himself wishing he was back in the cave, freezing and terrified like they were last night. *Who could have imagined that that terrible nightmare would soon seem like a dream come true?*

He tried with all his might to slip his hands from the cuffs, but they were too tight; they just dug deeper into his wrists. All he could manage was to shift his whole body even closer to Samira. He pressed the full length of himself to her, and kissed her. And kissed her again. And again.

If nothing else, he'd kiss her until the end of time, whenever that would be.

He heard a scrape at the side door and his heart lurched.

They were back already!

He heard a bang. The tinkle of glass.

A hand was reaching in through the broken window in the kitchen door! It was turning the knob!

When the door swung open, Cam almost laughed out loud in pure relief.

It was Dakota!

45

"**F**rickin' A," Dakota said. "This is nuts!" A crooked half-grin swept across his face. He stood over Cam and Samira, his hands on his hips, chuckling.

"Untie us!" Cam hissed. "They might be back any second!"

"All right, all right, cool your jets. I'm on it." Dakota bent and pulled a pair of garden shears from his back pocket.

"Found these suckers in the garage. Thought they might come in handy." He snipped the handcuffs from Samira's hands and feet first, then did Cam's. "OK, kick it!"

They scrambled to their feet. Dakota darted through the kitchen door. He beckoned to Cam and Samira to follow him, keeping close to the side of the house.

"Cormorant's truck is out front. Keys still in the ignition. We can get to it without being seen, if we stick close to the side of the house, then cut around behind the garage."

"We thought you had gotten shot!" said Cam.

"Keep your voice down," Dakota reminded him as they edged their way along the house wall. "No, I just decided to lay low. You see, my antenna went up as soon as you said this place belonged to Cormorant. And when you said he was a friend of your dad's...I mean, Christ! I know your dad! There's no way he'd be involved with this shit. But Cormorant! I knew he was up to his eyeballs in it...

176

"Between that and the choppers, man, I just got this hinky feeling. It said, 'Stay away, dude.' So I decided I'd do that, keep my options open, play it safe."

"Why didn't you say something?" Cam asked, wide-eyed.

"I tried! But you took off so fast, I guess you didn't hear me. Those choppers, man! Noisy buggers. Anyway, I doubled back toward the water. I didn't think the choppers had noticed me, but to be safe, I waded back into the river. I ducked down as deep as I could and still be able to see. I held my breath and watched. They passed right over me. I thought they were going to just keep going west, but then I saw them turn to the north and make a bee-line for you, Cam.

"That's when I heard something that sounded like shots, and I saw you start deking like mad. I was, like, 'Holy shit, what's going on?' I didn't know *what* to do—I was just totally freaking out. I thought you guys were dead meat for sure. But then the choppers turned around, headed back toward the mountains. That was one sweet relief, lemme tell ya.

"I couldn't be sure they wouldn't swing back again, though, so I stayed out of sight under the trees. I wanted to see what Cormorant was going to do. Depending, I'd either join you guys up at the house, or hotfoot it somewhere else. But just so you know, I wasn't gonna just leave you. No way. My antenna was tingling, after all.

"It was only a couple of minutes before those two dudes showed up. It looked like they were RCMP or something—I couldn't tell from where I was. But I figured it was a good sign. Everything was gonna be OK—Cormorant had called the cops.

But then I saw Cormorant take off in his SUV. *Now why would he do that when you and Samira were still there with the cops?* I wondered. I got that hinky feeling again, even stronger this time Then, when the cops came outside without you, I knew things were dead wrong, man. If nothing else, they shoulda been calling a squad car and hustling the two of you back to the station house. I mean, there were U.S. freaking border cops shooting at kids on Canadian soil, right? They shoulda been calling out the big kahunas, not just taking off and leaving you guys on your own."

They came around the corner of the garage. Even in the fading light of early evening, they could clearly see Cormorant's white pickup standing just a few yards away. At Dakota's nod, they ran the short distance to the truck and piled into the front seat. Dakota slid behind the wheel.

He flicked the keys that were dangling in the ignition, making them jingle.

"Man, that Cormorant is a douche, leaving his machinery like this," said Dakota, shaking his head.

"But where can we go? Who can we trust?" asked Samira.

"There's no one," Cam agreed, biting his lip. "This whole town is messed up."

Dakota grinned at him, a big fat cheese-eating grin. "Not true, my friend, not true! There is someone we can trust!"

"Yeah? Like who?" scoffed Cam.

"Like your dad," replied Dakota brightly as he turned the key.

46

The engine roared to life and the truck began to shudder and shake.

"Fricking thing needs a tune-up," Dakota said, swearing softly to himself. "Figures Cormorant doesn't look after his machinery, either."

"My dad?" said Cam, in total shock.

"Yeah, your dad."

Dakota released the truck's brake. Glancing toward Samira, he said, "By the way, this ain't gonna be pretty driving. I suck at it and my night vision is crap. So, sorry in advance."

Then he floored it.

The tires screeched and the truck leapt erratically down the drive. Bits of gravel clattered under the wheels and clanged against the sides of the truck. Dust rose behind them in a plume.

"Word's been going around that your dad's been working with the Mounties to help identify local grow operators," Dakota shouted over the noise. "That's what all of this is about, isn't it? The drugs?"

Cam nodded.

"Yeah. I knew it had to be. Once I realized Cormorant was involved."

"What do you know about my father?" Cam said. "Spit it out. Now."

"Nothing concrete, man, but people are talkin'. Have been for a long time. That's one reason why I had to stay away from you, buddy, once I started working for Cormorant. If your dad was a snitch—well, I couldn't exactly be hangin' with you now, could I?"

"I don't frigging believe it," Cam said. "I had no clue."

"Well, why would you? You're not exactly a subscriber to *The Grand Forks' Drug-runner*, eh?" Dakota replied.

They turned east on the Crowsnest Highway. Its surface caught the last rays from the dying sun, glowing like a pink ribbon against a blue-black night.

"*Yee-hah!*" Dakota shouted, gunning the engine. "Over the river and through the woods, to Cammy's house we go…!"

Cam could feel Samira's body tense inside the circle of his arm. He pulled her close to him, put his lips to her ear and whispered, "We're going to be OK! Just hang in there, a couple more minutes. That's all!"

Suddenly, a bright light was in Cam's eyes, blinding him. In the opposite lane, three cars with lights flashing and sirens blaring were racing down the highway toward them. Two more cars were parked on the road itself, blocking their passage.

Cam saw six police officers facing them, bracing themselves in the ready position. In body armour. Guns extended.

"What the—" said Dakota. "Dammit! This isn't good. Listen you, two—just shut up and let me do the talking, OK?"

Cam nodded grimly. Samira turned her face to his shoulder.

"Stop where you are!" he heard the order coming from a bullhorn. "This is Staff Sargeant Benniko."

180

Grand Forks's top cop!

"Park your vehicle on the side of the road and put your hands in the air!"

Dakota brought the truck to a stop on the edge of the highway. Cam reluctantly let go of Samira and put his hands in the air. Samira did the same, but Dakota kept his hands where they were—one on the wheel, and one on the stick.

They sat there, hearts pounding, mouths dry as dirt, surrounded by the smell of engine fumes and hot asphalt as the RCMP sergeant emerged from the closest car. Dakota let the engine idle as the sergeant approached. Benniko was a heavy-set man with a thick handlebar moustache and a toothpick between his lips. He was rolling it around between his teeth as he ambled toward them.

"Glad we managed to stop you kids before somebody got hurt. You were doing 120 in a 60 zone. And I bet you don't even have a driver's license."

Dakota smirked. Of course he didn't have a license. He wasn't even sixteen yet. But he didn't say a word.

"But now that I got you here, we can talk about an even more serious matter. I been getting reports about you two boys," Sergeant Benniko continued. "That you've been growing and running drugs. Frankly, I'm not surprised about you, Dakota. You've been making trouble ever since you were but knee-high to a grasshopper. But Cam. From such a fine, upstanding family as yours! Now I didn't expect that!"

"No, you have it wrong!" Samira interrupted. "It's Mr. Cormorant that's involved with the drugs! The man that lives in that house back there! Him and two of the Border Patrol guys."

"Yeah!" agreed Cam. "Officer French and Officer Hunko. They're his partners."

"Naaaah...you can't possibly mean Canada's finest are involved in criminal activity...and certainly not my old pal, Officer Lambert?" replied Benniko.

The squad car's passenger door opened. Hunko got out.

47

"Oh, shit," said Dakota. Then, "Hang on!"

He slammed his foot down on the gas pedal and released the clutch. The pickup's tires squealed as it sprang into motion.

"Pray like mad that your dad's home!" Dakota veered to the right, off the highway. He bumped along through the fields, aiming towards the river.

"What are you doing?" squealed Samira.

"If we can stay off the roads, they'll have a harder time catching us," he shouted back.

Cam hung on tightly to Samira. Dakota was driving like a crazy man, cutting corners and deking around shrubs, all the time staying in sight of the river and off the road.

It was less than a kilometre to Cam's house, but it was still too far away for them to make it. The police cars had turned around and were racing along on the Crowsnest Highway, parallel to the river. They'd get there first.

Dakota kept gunning the engine, trying to make the truck go even faster. But it was no use. The cops had the advantage.

Cam saw Dakota's eyes narrow.

"Hold on to your hats," he yelled. Then he spun the steering wheel sharply to the right. He was driving the truck straight into the river!

"What the hell?" shouted Cam.

"Get out! Get out!" Dakota yelled back. "We'll have to split up. Run for it! Hope they can't spot us in the dark! That's the only way!" Dakota leaned across Cam's and flung open the passenger door. "I'll lure them off your trail, then double back and catch up with you at the house. We're out of time. Go!"

Dakota threw all his weight against Samira, and pushed her with all his might. She and Cam tumbled out of the open passenger door to the ground. Dakota, meanwhile, tucked and rolled out the other side of the cab.

"Run!" Dakota yelled and pointed. Then he turned away from them and took off in the opposite direction.

48

"**S**amira! Stay with me!" Cam shouted. They ran as fast as they could through the long grass, heading toward a stand of trees near the creek that marked the western boundary of the Stewart homestead.

The *whomp! whomp! whomp!* of the approaching choppers was deafening.

"*You are surrounded. Surrender peacefully and you will not be harmed,*" an amplified voice commanded. It seemed like it was coming from everywhere at once.

Cam instinctively held his breath so as not to betray his presence. He crouched low, trying to flatten himself into the meadow. He reached for Samira's hand, laced his fingers through hers, and squeezed them tight.

"We have to get down to the creek," he said urgently.

Keeping his body low to the ground, he started to run, pulling Samira along with him. He kept his mind firmly on his goal—reaching the creek. He could hardly make it out; it was just a dark line against the even darker lines of hills and sky.

The noise, the wind, and the blinding lights all made Cam dizzy and disoriented. He couldn't tell if the throb in his chest was the reverb from the relentless beat of the chopper blades, or from the hammering of his own heart. He glanced up to check his bearings, and wound up looking right into a high intensity beam. Bright pink spots flared in his vision. Everything else went black.

"Cam? Those lights! I can't see a thing!" Samira wailed.

"Me neither. Hang in there. We're close. Just follow me, and stay low!"

Swearing softly to himself, Cam dropped to his knees. Now they would have to *feel* their way to the creek.

Tough grass slapped him in the face and filled his mouth with grime as he crawled commando style. He wouldn't have thought the world could hold even more terror when an ATV appeared out of nowhere. It swooped across the field at top speed.

Cam shrank into himself, willing himself to be invisible. The ATV seemed about to pass them by, when it made a sharp turn. Suddenly, its intense headlights shone right on Cam and Samira. They'd been caught!

"Run!" shouted Cam, knowing even as the words escaped his lips that it was too late. The ATV was bearing down on them. It was going to run them over!

There was nothing more to do. It was all over. Cam pulled Samira to him and covered her body with his own. He could feel her slight frame shaking beneath his. He closed his eyes and waited for the huge wheels of the ATV to crush them like roadkill.

The ATV roared past.

Squinting, Cam watched the ATV careen recklessly across the field, gears screaming as the engine was pushed to the max. The choppers swooped and dove overhead, their lights swinging crazily this way and that. Their furious blades battered Cam with blasts of hot wind. The gusts flattened the grass and flung stinging sand into Cam's face.

Then the search beams began to converge on the ATV.

As each searchlight latched onto it, the ATV's yellow paint seemed to glow brighter and brighter. To Cam, it looked like a chariot of fire against the night sky.

Standing tall on the machine, the driver was just an anonymous black shape silhouetted by the searchlights. He held his arms out to the sides like a crazy man.

One search beam caught the driver full on. His face was suddenly illuminated. Cam heard Samira gasp beside him. It was Dakota!

The ATV roared off, away from the creek. The searchlights stayed with it, tracking Dakota's path across the pasture.

"Run! Now!" Cam shouted. He and Samira both leapt to their feet. Shielded by the darkness, they sprinted toward the creek.

Cam had never run so hard in all his life. At last, the deep shadows ahead of them gained definition. They separated into individual shapes—the trees and bushes at the creek's edge. With lungs burning and every muscle on fire, Cam crashed through the tangled shrubs. Samira was right behind him. The moist fragrance of the creekbed rose up to welcome them. *They'd made it!*

Cam hurtled down the slope. When he skittered to a stop at the bottom, he bent over to help Samira to her feet.

A staccato burst of gunfire ripped through the night.

There was a flash of white.

A terrifying *whoosh* tore through the air, and a concussive wall of wind slammed into Cam, sending him staggering backwards.

Sudden understanding coursed through him.

"No! Don't look!" Samira begged.

But he had to look. Had to know.

What he saw made him want to puke. The ATV was a fireball.

49

Cam was too horrified and sick to move. But then Samira was at his elbow. Her voice in his ear was demanding, insistent.

"We have to get moving! Now!"

She tried to drag him away, but Cam couldn't take his eyes off the horrific scene.

"But Dakota…" he gasped. "I've got to help him!"

Samira's fingers grasped his chin. She forcibly turned his face toward hers.

"Nothing can save him now. Let's go. *Now!*" she insisted.

Cam snapped back to his senses. She was right. They had to get moving. And fast. There was nothing he could do for Dakota. But he could still save Samira and himself, as long as he didn't lose it.

Hand in hand, Samira and Cam ran along the creek, following the curve until it brought them directly behind the barn. Cam paused there to catch his breath and to figure out what to do next.

He said to Samira, "On the count of five, we gotta bee-line it for the kitchen door. It should be open—my mom never locks it. If Dakota was right and my dad's on the right side of this thing, we should be OK. He's home today. Or at least he should be. Wait—to be safe, I'd better check."

Cam squirmed up the damp creek bank on his belly. He pulled himself to the lip of the bank and peeked over.

Yes, his dad's truck was in the drive, just where it should be.

But so was Sergeant Benniko's car!

Cam let himself slide back down beside Samira.

"Not good," he reported. "Benniko is inside with my dad."

Samira bit her lip. "Now what?"

"I dunno," Cam said. "How about I do a little scouting to find out what's going on inside?" he suggested.

"But what if they see you?" Samira said, clutching at him, panic in her eyes and voice.

"This is my backyard, Samira. I know how to stay out of sight here. Believe me, I've had tons of practice."

"Cam, no! I don't want you to go!"

"I'll be fine," he said. He untangled Samira's arms from around his neck, kissed her fingers, and backed away from her. Then he dropped to his belly and began creeping through the grass.

It took him only a minute or two to reach the house. The windows of the front room were open—he could hear voices. Benniko and his dad. They were in the kitchen.

Silently, Cam made his way around to the back of the house. When he had reached the kitchen window, he slowly got to his feet, holding his breath, afraid to make even the slightest sound.

He peeped into the window.

Benniko was sitting at the kitchen table, facing Cam's dad. He was talking, and his father was listening carefully, a grim expression on his face. No doubt Benniko was spinning some kind of story, with Cam featuring as the villain...

Despite his better judgment, Cam threw open the kitchen door. He burst into the kitchen.

"Dad!" he yelled. "Don't believe him, whatever he says! He's lying!"

To Cam's surprise, his father bolted instantly from his chair. He threw himself across the table at Sargeant Benniko.

Something clattered to the floor. A gun!

It was sliding across the floor—right to Cam!

Cam bent to grab it, but his father got to it first. He scooped it from the floor and, in one smooth gesture, pointed it at Benniko's chest.

"Cam, call 911," he ordered. "Now!"

Cam's knees buckled. He felt dizzy. But his feet carried him across the kitchen to where the phone was mounted on the wall.

"You don't have to call anybody," said Officer French as he entered the room with Samira in tow. "We're already here."

50

"**W**ell it's about damn time!" said Cam's dad. "My arm was getting shaky."

"Dad! No! He's in on this thing with Benniko. And with Tommy! Tommy Cormorant!"

"No, I'm not, son," said Officer French. "I've been working undercover for a while. We knew Lambert was working with Cormorant, but we weren't sure who else was in on his scheme. We've been keeping an eye on Sergeant Benniko here for a while. We were building up a case against him and were about ready take action when all hell broke loose."

"Those biker dudes," Cam said dully.

"Yeah. Luckily, I had the chance to alert HQ of what was going down before anybody got shot. They've got those guys in custody now. Safe and sound."

"But Dakota…I saw the explosion…" Cam's eyes filled with tears. His legs went wonky. He wavered and almost collapsed, but his father reached out and put his arm around him, kept him upright.

"He's OK, Cam. The EMTs are with him. He's already on the way to the med centre."

"Don't lie to me! There's no way he's OK! I saw the ATV… the fire—"

"He jumped off the ATV before it was hit," said French. "Sent it racing into the creek as a decoy. Broke his leg and probably cracked his pelvis when he jumped, though. He's pretty banged up."

Samira's hands flew to her mouth and she burst into tears.

"I know, Sugar. It's a relief. We were all scared of what we would find out there. But I have some more good news for you. Your friends—the ones you were crossing the mountains with—are all safe. Our partner officers in the U.S. spotted the gang on Lone Ranch Creek Road in the National Forest over there. A truck was waiting on 'em. They took the whole bunch into custody. The traffickers are in jail in Washington State. Your friends are in a detention centre until the law can decide what to do with them. They'll probably be sent back to wherever they came from, but believe me, that's a better fate than they had in store for them here."

"Thank you for telling me," Samira whispered.

"You won't send Samira back to India, will you?" Cam blurted out.

"Now that's not really up to me," said Officer French, "but I might be able to pull a few strings to help her out. She's been such a big help to the Canadian law enforcement agency tonight, maybe we can work a little *quid pro quo,* so to speak."

"That's all fine and dandy," says Cam's father. "But now, we have this one here to deal with: Benniko." He spit the name out like it burned in his mouth.

"We're already on it," said French. A moment later, two RCMP constables came in and cuffed the Sergeant.

193

"Got an update for me?" French asked them as they hustled a scowling Benniko out the door.

"Yupper—we picked up Cormorant and Lambert. They're being processed at headquarters right now," said one of the constables. "And by the way, that officer from Immigration Canada you asked for? She's on her way now. She'll take your young lady into custody."

Cam's heart sank. He took Samira's hands in his and then pulled her close into a tight embrace.

"I don't want you to go," whispered Cam.

"I know," she said. "But we can still stay in touch, can't we?" She looked at Officer French for confirmation. He nodded at her.

"Sure," he said. "I'd hate to come between you two lovebirds."

Then he put his hand on Cam's shoulder, sighed heavily, and stepped out into the night.

Postscript

He had spent the next three weeks, pretty much, camped out in the waiting room of Kootenay Boundary Regional Hospital.

His dad stayed with him, most of the time.

Dakota had broken both his leg and his pelvis. But he also had a concussion, three broken ribs, and a collapsed lung.

The concussion was the worst of his injuries. The docs had figured he had gotten it when Joe Rocker kicked him in the head. But the damage was intensified when Dakota jumped from the ATV.

By the time he'd gotten to hospital, Dakota's brain had swelled so much he had to be rushed into ICU. They'd had to put him in an induced coma, to reduce further damage and help him heal. No one even knew for sure if he'd be OK when he came out of it. They'd all just have to wait and see.

While Cam and his father waited for the decree, they talked. It was something they hadn't really done much of for a long time, so the words, when they came, were rusty, brittle.

"I never meant to be so hard on you, son," Mike Stewart said, his voice unnaturally hoarse.

"You weren't," said Cam. "It was me that let you down. By disrespecting you. But not trusting you. By not pulling my weight."

His father had shifted uneasily in his seat. "Well, I suppose

195

I could say the same to you. That I didn't treat you with enough respect. Didn't trust you enough either. You know, it's real hard for me to remember you're not a little kid in your Batman pyjamas no more," his father continued, twisting his Lions' cap in his large hands.

"Truth is, you done good, Cameron. Real good. You oughta be right proud of yourself. You kept your head up there on the mountain. Made good decisions. Not a lot of men would have done what you did. Stand by that girl, get her down safe and sound."

"Thanks," Cam mumbled, eyes glued to the floor.

Then his dad excused himself, saying gruffly that he needed to go to the 'little boys' room.' It was a long time before he returned, and when he did, his eyes were red.

The doctors, when they finally came out, were jubilant.

"He's come out of the coma with flying colors. He's going to be fine," said the chief surgeon. "He'll need to be in traction for a few weeks more, for sure, and he'll probably never have a career as a boxer. But all in all, he was lucky. A scrapper, that one."

"You can say that again," said Cam as he gave his dad a high five, then surrendered to his father's bear hug.

Cam called Samira on his new cellphone. The one his dad called a "safety measure." Cam thought of it more as a peace offering.

Samira answered from her temporary home over in Midway. She'd been placed in foster care there until her case could be decided.

"So he's going to be OK," Cam said. "Maybe he'll have a gimpy leg, but all in all, the docs say he'll be fine."

"That's wonderful!" she said. "Really."

"How are you doing?" he'd asked her. "I miss you."

"I'm OK," she said. "Lonely. I spoke to my father. He still wants me to come."

Cam choked back his disbelief. "What? After he put you through already, he has the nerve to—"

"Cam," Samira interrupted. "He's my father."

Cam had glanced up at his own father, who was jingling his car keys, trying not to hurry Cam along, but communicating his desire to get moving all the same.

"They're all kinda pains in the ass, aren't they?" he said softly.

"I suppose," she said with a small laugh. "But they love us. And they're the ones we've got. Eh?"

Cam felt his face split in a wide grin when he heard the 'eh?'

"You're sounding like a Canadian already!" he told her.

"I'll take that as a compliment. But you know I'm just passing through, right?"

"Don't say that!" he'd said, alarmed. "They're gonna give you your papers—French as good as said so! Before you know it, you'll be a cheerleader at G.F.H.S., turning your nose up at an ordinary Joe like me."

Samira made a noncommittal click with her tongue. "All right, if you say so," she said.

"When will I get to see you?" Cam had asked her.

"Soon, maybe," she'd replied. "Depends on when Mrs. Szasz

197

will agree to drive me into town. She's pretty strict. Reminds me of my auntie in a way."

They'd talked for a while longer, but in the end, the conversation left Cam feeling unsettled, off balance.

So he wasn't surprised when, a few days later, Officer French stopped in at the Stewart home.

"I got the call this morning: Samira's disappeared," he'd said. "Slipped out of the house through a rear window. I been wondering—hoping, even—maybe she came to see you?"

Cam, felt the blood rush from his head. Everything seemed to telescope away from him and grow dim.

Had she done it? Gone over the mountains again, on her own?

He just shook his head *no* to all of Officer French's questions. Then he excused himself, locked himself in the washroom, perching on the edge of the tub until he heard French saying his goodbyes.

With his head in his hands, Cam rocked back and forth. *Had she cared so little about him that she could just take off without even saying goodbye?*

Cam walked around in a daze for weeks after that. Torn up with emotions he couldn't control, and couldn't understand. He hated her for leaving him. Loved her even more now that she was gone. But mostly he just worried about her, picturing her shivering in a cave like Ambar, dying alone.

But no—Cam knew that would never happen. Samira was too smart for that. Besides, she'd been better prepared than Ambar. Her foster family told French that their camping gear had disappeared along with Samira—the gear and a dozen eggs.

It was the third week of June, the last week of school. Cam was visiting Dakota in the hospital, like he did every afternoon, when his phone dinged. A text message had just come in. An unknown number.

The message simply said, "Don't worry. Safe in Seattle. On way to NYC by bus. AOK. I won't ever forget you XO –S."

"Holy crow," he'd said excitedly. "It's from Samira!"

"What's she say?" Dakota asked rising up on his elbows from his hospital bed.

"Screw off! I'm not telling you!" said Cam as he rapidly thumbed his reply: *Where r u? Call me!*

But his text bounced back. "Message undeliverable."

Cam stared at the words on the screen in disbelief.

How could she? How could she—?

"Dude! What did she say? Don't keep me in suspense!" Dakota tossed his empty pudding cup at Cam.

Cam ignored him. Instead, he quickly called the phone number that showed on his display, and chewed his cuticles as he listened to the phone ringing on the other end.

No answer.

He snapped the phone shut. Mixed emotions roiled inside him. Anger. Frustration. Relief. Despair.

Despite himself, he started to laugh.

"What? said Dakota. "*What?* You are killing me here."

She had *really done it*, Cam thought. *She had figured out how to be reunited with her dad. It's what she'd wanted all along, wasn't it?*

"She's on her way to New York," Cam said simply.

Dakota sagged back into his pillows. "Far out," he said. "So when you going?"

Cam looked up sharply. "Who, me?"

"Who the heck else, wanksauce? You *are* going after her, aren't you? You can't let a girl like that get away. Not a guy like you, anyways. She's the best thing you'll ever get, buddy, and that's the freaking truth." Dakota shook his head. "Nope. You better start packing, Cammo. And make sure you pass your damn road test fast. She won't wait forever."

"Piss off," Cam said as he reread Samira's message to himself. She'd said, "I won't ever forget you," right there in black and white.

He wanted to believe that more than he'd ever believed anything in his life. But people were funny that way. They did forget, no matter what they promised. But there was no way *he* would ever forget.

Cam lifted his eyes from the phone. He watched Dakota fidget with one of the bandages on his bad leg. Dakota was humming, painfully out of tune, "These vagabond shoes..." That *New York, New York* song.

Dakota really was a total dick. A good guy where it counted, maybe. But a colossal pain in the ass, no doubt about it.

Cam felt a smile starting to carve its way across his face. "So what do you, say, D? Up for a road trip to New York when they kick you out of here?" he asked.

Dakota turned his hugest, wacked-out smile on Cam.

"Awesome! Thought you'd never ask. We can call and reserve the penthouse suite at the Ritz. But how about *you* do the driving, this time, since I so *clearly* suck at it. Okay?"

to jump to
www.helainebecker.com

Creating Trouble with Author Helaine Becker

Where did the idea for *Trouble in the Hills* come from?

I was in Grand Forks, British Columbia, on a book tour sponsored by the British Columbia Library Association. Grand Forks sits right smack next to mountains that lie on the Canadian/American border. As I travelled through the area, I'd been hearing a lot about the problems with the drug trade. I had also been reading in the newspapers about human traffickers who had been caught going through those same mountains. Standing in the parking lot outside of the Borsht Bowl restaurant, the entire plot snapped into place in my mind. Everything that happens in *Trouble in the Hills* could indeed happen—all the background events in the book are based on facts, even though the story itself is pure fiction.

Have you ever been mountain biking?

I'm a pretty avid cyclist and have done a bit of mountain biking in British Columbia and Utah, but I'm no daredevil.

What was the hardest part of writing *Trouble in the Hills*?
Getting Samira right. I have teenage sons, so it was easy for me to hear Cam and Dakota in my mind. But to create a character from a different background and from the other side of the world and make her ring true was a challenge. Luckily, I had help from my good friend Mahtab Narsimhan, who was born in Mumbai. She helped me with Samira's speech patterns, mannerisms, and attitude.

What advice do you have for aspiring writers (or for kids who just have to write essays for school)?
The hardest part is getting started. Write anything—and I mean anything!—at the top of the page. Once you begin, it's easier for the words to flow. And once you have something down on paper, it's easier to correct what's there than to start from scratch.

Will there be any more books featuring Cam, Samira, and Dakota?
I've outlined two more plots for further titles. Whether those books get written or not will depend on how popular *Trouble in the Hills* is!

Helaine Becker is an award-winning writer of children's books with over 40 titles to her credit, including the best-selling *Looney Bay All-Stars* series, *Secret Agent Y.O.U.*, and *The Insecto-Files* (winner of the inaugural Lane Anderson Science Book Award for Children). Helaine lives in Toronto, Ontario. Visit her website at **www.helainebecker.com.**